Author

SOUMIK CHAKRABORTY

Soumik was born and brought up in Kolkata in a joint family with liberal values. After an eventful school life, he completed his engineering from Haldia. Despite being a Civil Engineer, he started his career as an IT professional with TCS, 10 years ago. Soumik has a great flair for writing and he penned down his first book 'My First Onsite' about the memorable experiences and adventures during his stay in United Kingdom for office assignment. He has a keen interest in travelling, playing guitar and he is addicted to gaming and football. His focus has always been on creating memories and unfurl his achievements.The endless domain of 'What if' is his favourite food for imaginative thoughts. Soumik goes by the Instagram handle Soumik_chk2410

Novel

SOUMIK CHAKRABORTY

Published By
Redgrab books Pvt. Ltd.
942, Mutthiganj, Prayagraj, 211003
www.redgrabbooks.com
contact@redgrabbooks.com

First published by Redgrab Books in 2020

Printed and bound in India
Cover Design & Typesetting by Redgrab Books team

ISBN : 978-81-94544-56-2

ACKNOWLEDGEMENT

Global Warming has always been that slow toxin towards humanity, which everyone is aware of, afraid of, but the fear of it never had that sting in it, to change any of ours ways of life. So much so that we human beings can't even give up plastic bags knowing fully well that even such a small sacrifice can save the next generations to come. I have always been fanatical about this conviction of everyone around me, that any small step from their side to fight this imminent danger will end up in vain, as our individual actions are minuscule when compared to the global scheme of things. I always believed that the Great War against Global Warming has to be inspired from individuals like us, through our daily actions and by making small sacrifices. Nevertheless, someone must step up and start that War.

This obsession of mine gave way to this book, the idea of a common man taking the reins in his hand and taking a step about it. A step in the wrong way as there were no right ways. I would love to thank the love of my life, Samraggi, for her strongest support all along the way, starting from mood swings to talking in my sleep about murders. I would also like thank my family and close friends who has been my constant support and encouragement throughout this journey.

Contents

CHAPTER 1

When criminals do it, it is a crime but when heroes are a part of it, it is Cloud 9 for Paparazzi's and front page feeders for the week, BREAKING NEWS clinchers in every TV channel and the hot cup cake for Facebook policing. This lasts only for a week or two max but Akash was having a super hard time handling it. He even thought about the disgraced bond of the blade and the wrist and the red ink to sign the lines but his burden of pending responsibilities chained his hand back. He could only drink Johnny and stare at the news, which had already deviated from the holy path of truth to the fruitful land of stories and with every new stretched truth, the TRP was rocking skywards, urging Akash to curse and say the golden mantra, which has kept his pulses beating till now. He poured the last drops of Johnny, Walked to the shelf and made another peg, gulped it and closed his eyes and sighed 'THIS TOO SHALL PASS', a long pause, out came 'Motherfuckers' and the glass danced on the ground and tore itself to pieces.

Akash Bose was an IIT Kharagpur graduate but his line of profession had no need of this degree. In fact, this particular uniqueness of his profession, which does not care of his flashy degree, was one of the main reasons why Akash was one of the most renowned private detectives in Bangalore. He was a Bengali by birth and was born and brought up in Kolkata. Growing up with Felu Da, Byomkesh, Kiriti and others, Akash was too obsessed about detectives from childhood. From an early age, he had this habit of thinking everyone around him to be a secretive 'Maganlal Meghraj' and would continue to scrutinize everyone around him, both known and unknown, for a dodgy behavior. If he managed to find any, at the first opportunity, he would share his findings with his mother who would buff it out or just say without looking at him 'Ahhh, well noticed, now please finish your apple' and continue watching the TV Soaps. No one had such a nose and hunger for suspicious behavior as Akash. His list of behaviors, each individually proving enough for one to serve a jail time, included (but not limited to)

Why would Samir Kaka return with an empty bag from market?

Badri Kaka is going from one fish stall to another, discussing something with everyone but has not yet bought anything!

That person has a cut in his forehead. That kind of mark cannot be caused by a cricket ball

Why is that boy and girl talking so secretively?

Why is the dog barking at that person, it does not bark at Akash, it only waggles its tail when he feeds his tiffin to them (This part was not informed to Mom).

Akash's parents thought that their only child's obsession was only childish and would fix itself once he grows up but their dreams were shattered when at the age of 10, Akash called the police when Sharmila Aunty came over to their house for the first time. He had caught her in the act, by peeping through the keyhole of their guest room. He immediately informed her mother about it, once, twice and thrice even, that Sharmila Aunty was not Sharmila Aunty, as the lady in the locked guest room had short hair while Sharmila Aunty had long hair. His mother only said while staring at the TV, 'Ohhh, good, ok finish your orange now'. He continued to poke her for the deserved attention to the grave matter, but no luck. He ran to his dad and explained the matter. Dad always listened but always missed the point. It's as if, Dad only listened to find a fault in Akash's behavior and though there were none to find, Dad would always make one up and slam him for that fault rather than understand the gravity of the incumbent danger. This time was no different. The tiny little mistake of peeping through someone's keyhole took priority above the imposter lady on the other side of the door who could change her length of the hair. Can you just believe that! Only Akash knew the pain of living with ignorant grownups with no Sherlock sense. Well, as the duty of keeping the family safe lied with him only, he would have to do the wrong thing for the right reason and so he peeped through the keyhole again.

The lady with short hair was pouring water in a glass, and another glass and another. How much water does this Aunty drink! She continued to add things from here and there to the 3 glasses and eventually took a medicine bottle, and opened it and poured something in all the 3 glasses. OH NO! POISON, she is going to poison Akash's family, what is he going to do. She is surely going to serve them as a special drink, kill them all, and run away with their money. What can Akash do to stop her, Mom would only make her have another fruit if he told her about the wicked woman's plan and Dad would kill him if he knew he peeped again. He could not make up what to do, how to save his family and just then, he saw the police patrol officer go by the street. Who said police never comes at the right time. God was with him and so God has sent the police. He quickly ran to the police uncle and told him about this aunty who is going to poison his family...... The rest, better not be said. Its one night Akash wants to forget but never can. Sharmila Aunty brought out someone else's hair (without the head! How did she get it?) in her hand and said that it's her Pig. Akash knew how a Pig looked like and the hair did not look like a Pig at all. He was pretty sure that Pigs don't even have hair. Sharmila Aunty also said that he was making them her most popular 'Adrak Lassi' and she kept the 'Adraks' in an empty medicine bottle. She also said she has never been so much insulted in her life. Akash also remembered that he had never had a Chappal Slap in his life (yet) other than that night.

Chappal slap was only the beginning; his parents took all his detective story books and started to raise the tone of their voice at the mention of anything fishy noticed by Akash. But it was too late, Akash already had access to internet in Dad's phone and continued to read all detective e-books secretly. This secretive indulgence to 221B Baker Street, 21 Rajani Sen Road and others only sharpened Akash's instincts. Years passed by and Akash was already a well-known smart ass in his friend circle. He would get cases of who stole Manas's rubber, who ate Raj's tiffin and when he went to higher standards, the standard of his cases increased to if Ria was double timing with Ganesh, were Gauri and Prem really in true love, what is their Chemistry teacher most afraid of etc etc. By College, Akash was the most well known problem solver in the town. Friends, Friends of friends and even cousins of friends came to consult their issues to Akash. Things were going good until IIT came to his life. He became too busy with studies and the pressure of it and soon after, got a desk job with a seven-digit salary in Bangalore.

In office, no one knew of Akash Holmes and frankly, no one cared. Akash surrendered to the stringent delivery timelines and board meeting preparations and the usual verbal abuses by his boss. He could not find any time to follow his heart but every time he got drunk, he blurted all his heart out, of the sadness that is developing inside him for not being able to act or read any thrilling detective novels. The rest of the night, he would torture everyone by repeating the same old stories of his solved cases and end up vomiting by the basin. Things turned into monotony, hence his colleagues started to refrain themselves from being a repeated listener of the drunkard. Akash's only passion turned into poison and left him without any friends to confine in. Sad and lonely, with no friends, Akash had only one thing to do – office work – and so he dedicated all his time into being good in that. The more he performed, the more his boss gave him work till the time that Akash became too stressed and had to be hospitalized.

He did not need a Doc to tell him this as he very well knew, but still, the Doc did, re-confirming that he was suffering from extreme depression and the only way out of this was mental piece, no stress and he prescribed a month of leave from office. Finally, he had some time to rub the dust of his book collections and read them one by one. Slowly, that inner piece was rejuvenating. One evening, he got a call from an unknown person, Ehsaan, who had his number from one of Akash's friend and he wanted to meet him. When they met, Ehsaan told him that he thinks his wife is cheating on him and he needs proof to file for a divorce. He also added that he was afraid to go to any official private detectives. He had heard from his friend about Akash's passion for finding out the truth and he has also heard that Akash has some free time now. The icing on the cake was when he said that he could pay Akash a fee if he can find proof. Akash thought of getting up on the table and jumping in joy but restrained himself to negotiate the fees and exchange further details of the case.

The next week was one of the best that Akash had for a long time. He was pursuing someone, and that too with a non-romantic purpose, the thrill of ensuring that he does not get caught, wearing fake beards and moustaches, bribing others to get information's and using his deduction powers to strategize his next move to catch the dame in the act. After 10 days, Akash finally had cumulated all the evidences and in a proper bookish manner, he called Ehsaan to his flat, provided him with details of her wife's movements, whom she was dating, how she got around it, the other mobile phone she uses to call him and last of all, PDA photographs. Ehsaan cried while Akash rejoiced in the manner he played the endgame.

Akash had never felt so rejuvenated. With this success, he started to get more clients, all just wanted to check their spouse's loyalty. As Akash was not a proclaimed private detective, he was easier to approach for the common people and his name had spread already, as he was an IITian loyalty detective, a very rare combination. Akash no more wanted to work in office and lost his focus from office work, he started to miss targets in office while his detective investigation targets of two in a month were easily met. He had to work overtime in his personal detective agency, which meant more and more sick leave in office. Soon, he received his first warning from office but Akash just shrugged it. He had already suffered enough to understand that a desk job could never quench his thirst, so he put all his focus on doing something he is passionate about rather than run for a higher package. He was determined, never to get depressed again. So, as Akash did not pay any attention to the second warning he received too, his company soon sacked him. Akash did not care if he had a 9 to 5 job. He was an IITian after all and that too with a job experience. He can get into office life, any day he wants but if he stopped his loyalty test entrepreneurship, he knew that his name would soon fade away from people's mind and he would never be able to enjoy his work again. Now that he did not have a 9 to 5 job, he would take more cases and with each success (failure of someone's marriage), his catalogue would improve and attract more and more spouses.

As this continued for few years, at the age of 35, Akash was a 5ft 10in presentable view. He had an Amitabh Bachchan style beard (only his was still black) which went well with his long, crisp edged face, with cheek bones showing out on both sides. He had beautiful bluish eye balls like a cat and his hair was neatly cut but looked stylish. He had transformed well from his skinny office days to a slim, muscular body structure. He always dressed in suits which he was particularly fond of. His portfolio of solved cases now included few thefts, an escaped prisoner and document forgery apart from the huge list of nuptial divorces. He had yet to put the golden ring of solving a murder crime in his fingers. The police in few petty matters had consulted him but he craved to be more and more involved into justice.

Akash's ultimate sacrifice, leaving his 9 to 5 job in preference to the most unusual job, never went well with his parents who cut off all connections with him. His mother would still call him sometimes secretly but his father could never come to terms with Akash's career choice and never spoke to him again. This meant that Akash had to stay back in Bangalore as he had no one to go back to in Kolkata. The story of the IITian private detective could not have evaded from media and so, with every minute success, the media would make a story out of it. The media coverage would center on the point of how one man followed his heart and actually is doing well for the society. Akash often wondered what 'well' was he doing for the society? He was only doing well to his pocket but if the media mis-interpreted, that also went well for the pocket, so he did not try to literate the illiterates but continued playing his part whenever media attention was available. His fame was slowly catching its flames but all was about to change now.

Akash had handled so many divorce cases and seen how loyalty has gone in the drain these days, that, he refused to get married. He considered himself too emotional to handle a sexual betrayal from his wife. But Akash did have his fair share of erotic pleasures throughout adulthood due to his looks and a personal flat where any one can spend a one night stand but Akash avoided any sexual relationship with any married woman as he believed that there should be a unity among men to honor another man's love. Anyways, options were abundant and so, why go for the ones who are already officially taken. But soon, all his rules and ethics were about to break.

CHAPTER 2

As the glass danced on the floor, Akash could hear his own curse echoing through the room. The TV presenter shouted 'Self-proclaimed Private Detective Akash Bose sacrifices truth for lust.' The Breaking News tab covering the bottom of the screen flashed 'BREAKING NEWS – 'Cheat'-ective Akash Bose cheated truth to sleep with a criminal.' 'LIE! LIE! LIE!' Akash shouted at the bright box, enraged with pain, agony and watery eyes. 'I was fucking trapped….you assholes' and he remembered how Mrs Damini Roy came to Akash few months ago with a unique case in hand.

In an orange sari, which matched with her lipsticks, her round face features looked quite beautiful and her cat eyeglasses added that tint of hotness to her beauty. Her nose ring went well with her pointy nose and her jewelries betrayed that she belonged to a rich family. Underneath the entire make up to hide it, Akash could still see a fade of dull injury marks below her left eye. Akash understood that someone has physically tortured her and immediately, his heart melt. How can someone hit this angel. Damini came to the point straight away. She said that she got Akash's contact from the papers and would pay Akash well enough if he can gather proof of her husband torturing her. Akash was stunned in the emotionless manner she said that statement and that awe must have been clear in Akash's expression as looking at him, she got embarrassed and calmed down her tone and said 'I may have sounded rude but I have been physically abused by my husband for about an year now as I cannot give birth to a child. My womb cannot support a baby. It has been tough for Shankar to accept this and he comes home drunk every night and will force me to…….' A silence followed, the tears dropping down her cheeks filled the unsaid words. Akash did not know what to say but he need not say anything as Damini continued 'And if I resisted on few nights, he would…..would….. would hit me and RAPE me. Till I get pregnant, this will continue every night and I cannot take it anymore' she was howling now.

Akash stepped forward to console her and as Akash came near, Damini hugged him like a child hugs his mother when she gets hurt. Akash felt a strong hatred for Shankar, whom he did not even know. The hug tightened but the red light for tears just would not turn on. He consoled her all he could and even lifted her beautiful face, took it in his palms and assured that it will be quite easy for him to film this if this is a daily affair. This did the worse as Damini cried more and more, getting reminded at the looming torture for that night. Akash cursed himself to have delivered the worst line possible in that scenario to console her and just tightened his arms around her, as if, trying to choke her to stop crying. To Akash's astonishment, the choke worked, but again, in a different way than he expected as Damini was now responding to the hug and kind of, finding solace in Akash's arms. She too hugged him back and both of them had a moment there. Akash had this irresistible desire to kiss her out of her pain. He was sure that it would work like a charm just as the choke did but his profession ethics denied him of the privilege to have a sexual relationship with his client. It was a big dilemma for Akash. FUCK ETHICS or FUCK HER! Akash did not get a chance to make a decision as Damini herself realized the borders and straightened herself. The rest, she kept it very brief as she was getting too weak at Akash's presence. She handed over some advance money, along with her address, mentioned the time around which her husband would return home and then she left. A panting Akash was only left, asking for more, if it was left to him, his ethics would have gone down the drain by now.

Within that night, Damini had called Akash four times for silly reasons like what he was doing, what he ate at lunch and all those lover stuffs. Akash got the vibe but did not mind. He felt an invisible Cupid stinging him with arrows but he had a big job at hand. He had to stop Shankar's torture and the best way was to provide a video proof, which would be the doom of Shankar in their divorce case. By 9 pm, Akash had positioned himself in the place where Damini pointed out. It had a very clear view of the drawing room but it was too far to hear anything. Damini had said that their neighbors can alarm Shankar of Akash's presence if he was too close. Anyways, a video without audio would be enough of a proof to scare Shankar from further devilish nights and get the divorce. The devil came at 9.30 pm as Damini had informed and Akash began shooting. Shankar looked so polite, he thought. Akash continued to think that the lean lanky figure of Shankar with a very innocent face did not betray what lied beneath the face but he is going to uncover that soon and relief Damini of all her pains. Soon, Akash could see a the couple arguing about something. Both of them were putting their hands up in despair often and eventually, it happened, Shankar hit Damini with a tight slap and continued with three more till blood trickled through Damini's nose. Akash felt like running to Damini and hug her again to relinquish her of her pain but all he could do was, sulk his face ground wards, pack his camera and leave.

Akash had seen Damini's pain real time and already developed a soft spot for her. He was in regular contact with Damini now in context of discussing the case but they discussed everything except the case. Soon, the divorce case followed. Shankar turned out to be a very affluent media reporter and had multiple contacts in all levels. He hired a very credible lawyer and the lawyer constructed a new story that Damini had an extramarital affair, which Shankar had found out on the night of the video, and hence he hit her out of rage of betrayal. He also conjured multiple paid witnesses who lied about how innocent a character Shankar was and he can never hit a fly, leave alone his wife. Things were going southwards for Damini and her divorce case. Akash had to help her. He loved her and they can only be together if this divorce progressed well. Akash could not bear watching Damini cry on his shoulders every day and he felt helpless. This case had already gathered full media attention due to Shankar's affluence in media world and Akash's little but growing fame. Akash knew that they were staring at ending up on the losing side if he did not do anything soon. It's a very tough war always between ethics and mind, which to choose? However, when it's between ethics and heart, Akash knew that he would have to use his mind and listen to his heart and keep the ethics on the back seat for a while. Even Shankar's lawyer was bringing in paid witnesses and so he can do away with one too. He asked Damini's lawyer to inform judge that they are filing for divorce as Shankar was impotent. The lawyer obliged like a puppet. After a lot of drilling and media shaming, the Judge called for an impotency test. Akash used his sources and paid the lab reporter five lac rupees to issue a fake impotency certificate for Shankar and they won the divorce case on impotency grounds.

Akash was ecstatic. He can finally be with Damini but Damini was busy wrapping up the divorce case and get separated from Shankar, so Akash waited. Shankar was heartbroken. He was too much media shamed in the last few months to go back to media line again and he was trolled all around for impotency. Akash did feel very guilty about it but he consoled himself by accepting that he had no other options to win the case. However, this guilty feeling soon turned in to remorse. Shankar was a media person. He knew his ways around cameras and specially was good at doing a sting operation. A sting operation is exactly what he did, on his own wife, Damini, a drunk Damini, on the last day of their living under the same roof. Damini already got the alumni money and so she thought that she had won everything. Shankar proposed a parting away party among the two of them only and Damini got too drunk and confessed everything, and all the things she confessed was news for Akash too as he heard it in shock for the first time, from Damini's mouth, only that she was not near Akash, she was talking from the TV. Shankar took the help of his media friends to broadcast Damini's confession to the whole of India. Akash listened in shock and agony as Shankar pulled the topic of why Damini betrayed him when he was so loyal.

A drunk Damini was screeching in remorse in the TV as she told Shankar, how she had continued her relation with her old boyfriend, Samir, even after she was forcibly married to Shankar as Samir was from a different caste. Akash thought, funny how a crying girl could bring righteousness to extramarital affairs too. Damini carried on that Shankar was not at all a loving husband but never ever physically tortured her. As his reporting job kept him on long trips away from home occasionally, Damini was too bored with their married life. The way Damini explained, with her tears rolling down from beneath her glasses, it seemed very logical that Damini had no other way out of her boredom than to contact Samir, cry on his shoulders, and share her pain. She explained how her hands were trembling when she dialed Samir's number for the first time and how she disconnected the line multiple times without a ring, just for loyalty to Shankar. But it had mistakenly rang once and Samir called her back and she could not help but burst out about her strained married life. Samir always listened to her and she would feel much lighter after sharing her pain with Samir. They had initially decided not to meet and continue their 'friendship' over phone only but within two weeks, during Navratri, Damini could not bear to stay alone and broke the conditions of friendship by meeting Samir at a café. They had a fantastic time with Damini having a good laugh after a long time. They even went to the movie together where Samir tried to catch hold of Damini's hand but she would not let him. This went on for two more weeks when they went out a couple of times but Damini had decided they would never meet in enclosed structures again as it was becoming more and more difficult for her to resist the shameless approach of Samir to hold Damini's hand. Damini would shiver whenever Samir's fingers would touch her fingers and she would quickly close her fingers but Samir always maintained touch on her skin.

One night, Samir got drunk and came to her door and she had no options but to let him in, in fear that any of the neighbors might see him. This time, it was Samir crying in her shoulders as Samir explained how helpless he feels that he cannot help Damini out of her marriage and how bad he felt when Damini left him to marry someone else, just for money! Damini explained that she did not want to leave him at all, never for any amount of money. She also explained how her family forced her to marry Shankar as Samir was from a different caste; Samir said 'So, do you still love me! Do you still want to be with me, just like you promised to me every time we made love?' Damini did not have an answer to this awkward question, she wasn't prepared for it and silence was a provoking answer. Samir seized her hand tight and said 'Then why don't you like my touch anymore! Why don't you close your eyes when I touch you, when I kiss you here, anymore' and he kissed her beckoning neck. Before Damini could think anything else, her eyes shut automatically as she opened her neck wider for Samir. As Samir took a bite at it, she reacted by closing her neck to Samir's chin and she felt a warmth below her waist. Samir whispered in her ears 'Don't you remember how I used to whisper in your ears how beautiful you are and how I like it when you have goosebumps like you are having now!' Samir moved his lips from her right ears to her left neck and caressing the neck, he went on to suck her ear lobes and slowly and slowly whisper romantic lines into her ears. This used to be the sign that Samir wants to make love to her and always, Damini would follow the lead smilingly but not this time. Damini still tried to resist by trying to push Samir away with her right hand but the strength in the push was not forceful enough to move even a fly. Samir dropped his right hand to second base. As he moved his fingers from above her nighty over her breasts, the resistance game was over. Damini never wore a bra at home and that night was no exception. It became easier for Samir to breach beneath her dress and move his fingers upward as Samir whispered 'I have never felt your nipples so strong in all this time, so this is how much you want me Jaanu?' He kissed her lips with his until Damini surrendered to her abdominal juicy instincts and finally, tasted his lips after three long years. The rest of the night was spent by thrashing the borders of friendship in all ways possible. Shankar only listened in silence, without any show of any emotion except adding occasional fillers to the conversation with some jargons like 'Hmm' and 'Then?' to keep Damini's confession running.

Damini continued that although she always felt bad for letting Shankar's trust down, but she could not stop the guilty pleasures and wanted to run away with Samir and start a new life. She had to get a divorce but was too afraid to ask for one. She was afraid of what everyone else would think and then decided that the only way to get a divorce would be to put the blame on Shankar. But Shankar was too nice a person and had no faults worthy of a divorce. So, she came up with a plan. She saw Akash's name in the paper, as Akash was young, and can be seduced, reached out to him. She hit herself with a brick so that she can have a strike mark. In her confession she did not give the full description of what happened but only said. 'Things went just as she wanted with Akash and the night of the video, she intentionally kept Samir's under garments in the sofa.' Akash now realized that on the day of the video, Damini repeatedly called her to keep him distracted from doing any kind of background checks on Shankar. Akash furiously said 'Bitch!' Shankar found the under garments and as she expected, got enraged at her betrayal. When Shankar asked more and more questions, Damini provoked him by saying that Samir can satisfy her in the bed which Shankar cannot and started giving every small little details of how Samir pleasured her. Shankar was boiling with rage and the last nail in the coffin was when Damini showed all the love marks that Samir had given her and pointed to their bed's edge where Samir was making love to her when she got the love marks. Shankar fell in Damini's trap by not being able to control himself and slapping Damini for the first time ever. Damini reveled in the sweet pain, knowing that she can have her freedom now. Now, Akash realized why Damini acted a love story with him as Damini needed a puppet to work the case around, so that Akash does not believe the truth shared by Shankar's lawyer.

Damini had pursued the divorce case without Samir's knowledge and when Samir came to know about the divorce case, he got scared. Samir was actually cheating on Damini as Samir had already got married after Damini left him but did not inform Damini about his marriage. During the divorce case, when Samir came to know about it, he finally confessed to Damini and said that he has no plans to leave his wife. He was just using Damini for physical pleasure. Damini was heartbroken and had no one to love her anymore. She only cried and cried in Akash's arm when the divorce case was going on. Akash misinterpreted this to be her frustration with the marriage but in fact, the frustration was with her life and how Samir betrayed her. She also confessed in the video that Akash forged the impotency documents and then finally ended the video by asking for forgiveness and confirming that she would go away to New Zealand to her uncle as she had nothing left over here.

The media took this news by storm. It was the most trending news at that time. It was as if the journalists were resonating for justice for one of its family member, Shankar who had fought for justice and finally brought out the truth. Akash had become the scapegoat in this entire ordeal and the reporters were looking for his head all around. He could not go out of his house anymore as the media was all around, asking disturbing questions about his relation with Damini and built up fluffy stories and broadcasted it as breaking news. Akash was too afraid to pick up his phone and face anyone. So, he had no other option but to switch it off. He could not think of facing his parents now with all this allegations and his face flashing in every channel and newspaper. He suddenly became the most hated man of India, all because, Damini had played with his emotions. Akash's rage knew no bounds but Damini had already left for New Zealand, so he did not have any channel to exhale that rage and it sat like a devil inside of him.

CHAPTER 3

Indian high court takes oaths very seriously. Akash had taken an oath in the court not to lie and then blatantly lied to the court about the impotency. He even had forged evidences. The lady with the blind fold was not going to turn a blind eye on that one. Akash regularly went to the local police station and was questioned by police on how and why he forged the documents. The branch inspector, Mr Dhole, 44, was a friend of Akash through his detective work and understood that Akash was betrayed by Damini and he also understood why Akash had to forge the documents but the media was sitting right on top of the case and he could not act lenient. 'Janta ki Adalat' had already sentenced Akash to life imprisonment but the court's hearing was due soon and Mr Dhole was weaving the web for a lighter punishment on Akash. Mr. Dhole was a sluggish, lethargic police inspector with a big heart. He liked his duties to follow his own pace and hated timeliness in activities. He would work the case out with Akash and his lawyer often and one day when they were having this session in the police station, a mid-aged lady, came running towards Mr. Dhole and after a second or two of catching her breath, explained in very brief that her husband is missing and has not returned home for the last 2 days. While Mr. Dhole asked her to relax, Akash took a good look at her. She was wearing a dull salwar, she had no make-up, she definitely had been crying a lot this days as his eyes were red and fluffy. She looked to be aged at about early 30s and definitely belonged from a very rich family as her bangles were all original gold and her hair was permanently straightened and she was wearing a GUESS watch. She must have been married for 2 or more years as the look of the new bride had completely not been drained off yet. As the lady took her seat and gulped a glass of water, she voiced that she is Mrs. Haseena Khan and her husband has not returned home for two nights. His phone is switched off and none of his friends have any news on Mr. Khan's whereabouts. Mr. Dhole offered her coffee which she did not take nicely as this was not the response she was expecting. She was about to shout back at the insensitive response from the police officer but Mr. Dhole understood that now was not the mood for pleasantries and opened a big registrar and started asking the template questions of a missing case.

Just when Mrs. Haseena had said that Mr. Khan was a wood merchant, based out of Bomanahalli, Akash interrupted 'Are you referring to Mr. Khan, the famous wood merchant, CEO of Bangra Industries?'

Mrs. Haseena and Mr. Dhole, both diverted their face and attention to the convict, Akash Bose.

Mrs. Haseena looked both angry at being interrupted and happy that his husband was so famous and answered in affirmative and followed up with expectant eyes 'Have you seen him recently, do you know where he is now?'

Mr. Dhole also looked expressively at Akash. If Akash knew anything about Mr. Khan, his work would be easier and he can go to lunch much quicker as he was already starving. Akash only said that he knows a lot about Mr. Khan as he did a thesis upon him during his college days in a study of successful entrepreneurs from their Start-ups. He continued that he was inspired by Mr. Khan's success story as he had to go through so many rough patches and financial losses in initial days of his entrepreneurship journey to finally make it big which made Akash a big admirer of Mr. Khan. This instigated Akash to know more about Mr. Khan's daily life, his likes and dislikes, his habits, his background and how he turned himself into a business tycoon. Akash's sudden excitement on the situation of a missing person was not taken well by both of the other parties and hence, none asked any further questions to Akash about his thesis and Mrs. Haseena continued.

'My husband has not returned home for two days now. He last left home at around 8.30 pm day before yesterday, citing personal work. He said he has to meet someone and sort things out. He even took a lot of cash with him, which makes me doubt that he must have went to settle someone's payment related to business.'

'Sort things out! Is this the exact words he used?' asked Akash, to Mr. Dhole's surprise.

'Yes, Sort things out, that's what he said'

'Ok, then any further news?'

'Well, I tried to reach him once at 9.30 pm to know if he is going to have dinner. His phone rang but he did not pick up. I tried again around 10 pm and his phone has been switched off ever since. I have contacted all his friends and office staffs but none could give me any news.'

'Mr. Dhole, I think we should track the last known telephone signal of Mr. Khan, and Mrs. Haseena, have you checked Mr. Khan's private diary or calendar in his room? He has the habit of maintaining important dates in either a diary or his room's calendar as he did not trust mobile systems much.'

Both the other parties were quite surprised by Akash's knowledge and dictating approach. Mrs. Haseena said 'No I did not check those places but you are right, he does not trust mobile technology at all. How did you know he maintains this kind of records and where he maintains it?'

Akash just smiled and said, 'In IIT, you have to be very descriptive about your thesis subject and so, I gathered as much knowledge as I could of him.'

'Did you ever meet him?' asked Mrs. Haseena and Akash responded in affirmative 'Yes I could manage a 15 minutes interview with him few years ago but I am sure he won't remember me but I surely will remember him always. There were so many things to learn from him.'

Mrs. Haseena smiled for the first time in the afternoon and looked at Mr Dhole and asked 'So, what shall we do inspector?'

A hungry Mr. Dhole chanted the routine steps 'Well, we will put the phone on tracking, please leave his pictures with us so that we can circulate and we will file a missing report and let you know once we have any news.'

The convict, Akash said 'We should go look for clues in his home Sir. If a person is not mobile friendly, it means he could have left something behind in his house which can give us a clue where he went?'

Mr. Dhole was fuming at Akash for poking his nose too much into this case and he was in no mood to take advice from a person who openly lied in court. He strictly said, 'Look Akash, there are some formalities and protocols which we need to follow as police officers. We will do some investigation at our end, get the required paper work up and running, check through informers, do a background check and accordingly proceed with the case. We just can't go to someone's house suddenly.'

As Akash was about to apologize, Mrs. Haseena said 'I think your fellow colleague here is correct. We should start from our home where there might be something I have missed.'

Mr. Dhole corrected the understanding and said 'He is not our colleague, he is a private detective and he is facing a trial……'

Akash interrupted quickly 'Even better, as I am a private detective, I do not need to follow your paper work and I will go with Mrs. Haseena to their home and inform you of whatever I can find.'

Mr. Dhole exploded out from his chair with anger as Akash was trying to dictate him of what he should do. He was actually trying to disgrace the police's way of working and he was not going to tolerate that. He said 'Listen Mr. Akash Bose, the police does not need your help here. You can keep your knowledge to yourself as you have no say in this case. You are not related to this case in any way and you better stay out of it. We know our duties very well and we will do all we can to find Mr. Khan. You have no business here, please stop poking your nose into this matter.'

Both Akash and Mrs Haseena were taken aback by this sudden aggression for so less a reason. As Akash took it to be a mood swing due to hunger and was about to apologize, Mrs. Haseena knew that Akash was a well-wisher and revisiting their home was actually a good idea which the police will take decades to do by their process and she sharpened her voice and said ‘As Mr. Akash is a private detective, from now on, I am hiring him for my case to find my husband. Now does he have enough rights to suggest the best way forward for this investigation, officer? Now does he have the right to express interest and urgency to find my husband? From the moment I came in, he seemed much more logical and knowledgeable about this case and hence I am happily assigning him the case and he would be my representative. Now can he go with me to search our house and let you know if he finds anything?’

Now it was the inspector’s turn to be taken aback by the sudden aggression and he just said ‘You are misunderstanding me Madam, I had no issues with him reporting to me his findings but I would have liked my men to do that first as they are better trained than him and has better chances of finding a clue. But if you insist, I would not mind with Mr. Akash providing us information’s but we would be carrying out a search of your property soon too Madam? Now if you please excuse me, we shall be in contact. Also, I would recommend that you know whom you are hiring as this man has lied to the court in his last case and is facing court trial for this. No offence Akash.’

Akash nodded his head and said ‘None taken’ but Mrs. Haseena looked at Akash strangely, as if she suddenly regrets her decision but then turned back towards the police officer and retaliated ‘Thanks for all your help officer, hope to hear from you soon and the only thing I am interested in his past is his knowledge about my husband and whether that can help find him.’ Then she turned to Akash and said ‘Let’s go Mr. Bose’

When Akash was in Mrs. Khan’s car, he said ‘The way this works is I normally take an advance before I start to work on any case but the way you shut him up in the police station was more than I could have asked for. Thanks for standing by my side and I will not let you down.’

CHAPTER 4

This was Akash's first missing case and so he was rightfully nervous about all of it but he could not afford to show it on his face. He just maintained a straight look throughout the drive and rehearsed the scenarios for which one can be missing; accordingly, he needs to frame his questions. The thing about detectives is that the one you are questioning is not bound to answer you, unlike police, and so you need to place limited questions in a limited span of time. None of your questions should be offensive but only offensive questions fetch meaningful clues, so all the questions Akash can throw needs to have the harmony of time, relevance, revealing and directive to the events. Akash already knew that they lived in a joint family with an older and another younger brother of Mr. Khan. As they approached their home, Akash recognized the three-storied building he had once stalked. Each brother occupied one floor and there was a large garden in front of the building, which was well utilized by the children as their playground. The security guard opened the gates. Akash looked at him with suspicious eyes but he had still not learnt the art of hiding his suspicions. Mrs. Haseena caught his eyes and understood. She said that she will make tea for Akash while he can have a word with the watchman. Akash stepped down to discuss with the watchman about this issue. The watchman informed that he had last seen Mr. Khan leave the house at the same time as Mrs. Haseena explained. He left with his Enfield and not his white Toyota car. The watchman also informed that Mr. Khan used to take the bike only when he had to travel through the city or went to a nearby area. Akash asked if the watchman has seen anyone lurking around the house, to Akash's astonishment, the watchman said that now that he is being asked, he has seen a biker passing around multiple times a day in the last week. The biker used a black bike and black helmet. No clues there, Akash thought! As there would be a million bikers matching that description and he might have seen multiple bikers and confused them as the same person. Watchmen have the tendency to make stuffs on their own. The last question he asked the watchman was about the relation between the brothers to which the watchman said that all looked fine from his position. The watchman was not the 'dagabazz' types, 'One loyal fellow, my best source of information is an useless loyal slave, would not even tell me of the domestic drama' Akash cursed the watchman in his mind and went inside at the temptation of the tea.

As he went in the house, Mrs. Haseena introduced Akash to Mr. Abul Khan, 36, the older brother. As he took a seat, Akash faced towards Mr. Abul, took a good look at the older brother. Not attractive by any means, Abul looked more like a union leader than the regional manager, the post that he held in Mr. Khan's company presently. A distinct feature about his face was his nose. It was swollen as if hundreds of bees had tested their stings on Mr. Abul's nose only, and left the rest of the face untouched.

Lowering his rimless glasses, Mr. Abul broke Akash's stare by asking 'Bhabhi said that you are here to help to find bhaiya! Have you seen him? Do you know where he is?'

Akash did not know where to begin and felt lost for words. Finally he found some, but those were properly inappropriate 'Where were you when Mr. Khan got kidna.... I mean, missing.'

There was a sudden change of the atmosphere. Mr. Abul rudely stood up from his seat and said 'Kidnapped! What do you mean? And what has it got to do with where I was at that time? How dare you ask me that question? Who are you? Who has given you the right to ask me such a question and who told you bhaiya got kidnapped?'

Akash cursed himself and said to himself 'Asshole, now fix this.'

Akash also got up and was about to start explaining that he is a stupid rookie detective and this was his first interrogation session and he was tensed, but fortunately, Mrs. Haseena rushed to the scene from the kitchen to save Akash. God only knows what would have happened if Akash actually said those lines.

'Akash Bose is a private detective whom I have hired to help us find him. He is been missing for two days now, it is high time we accept that he may have been kidnapped and we have to take some steps about it. I feel suffocated every moment we just sit around hoping he would show up at the doors. We have to do something.' Commanded Mrs. Haseena.

'Bhabhi, main samaj sakta hoon but why a private detective! We could have taken help of the police, I can call the Deputy Commissioner and...'

A fourth voice suddenly exclaimed with much concern in his voice 'Police! Why police!'

Mrs Haseena gently pinched the introduction in between the heated conversation 'Akash, this is Raheel, my younger brother in law, he is a CA and looks at the accounts of the company.'

Although Akash turned towards Mr. Raheel to introduce himself but Mr. Raheel did not even look at Akash and did not seem interested. He had bigger concerns and showed no signs of composure in his voice 'The first thing police will do is look at the accounts of the company. We will be in deep trouble if it happens, there is a lot to be covered up before we can expose the accounts, you must understand Bhabhi.'

Like twin siblings, Mr. Abul reciprocated by copying Mr. Raheel's tone 'Yes Bhabhi, we must think about that before we involve police and....'

But Mrs. Haseena was the main deal in the house and it was quite evident through her temperament as she interrupted Mr. Abul 'And that is why I did not involve the police, I know that your brother would not like that too and that is why I have not involved them yet but we have to do something about it and so I hired a private detective and not the police.'

Mr. Raheel still ignored Akash as if he was a ghost 'But is he good? Will he be able to really help us?'

'There is no harm in trying and I have faith in him. He can only succeed if all of us help him, so lets co-operate with him. He would like to talk to both of you first. I will make tea for all of you' this were Mrs. Haseena's parting words before she left for the kitchen, leaving Akash exposed to the doubtful glares of the two siblings.

Akash finally felt relaxed to see both of the siblings sit down by the couch. He has the rare chance to start fresh with his interrogation. This time, he courteously asked how many children did they have and who else were there in the family. Abul informed that their parents had passed away two years back and only Abul had a 2 year old daughter. Abul and Raheel, both were Engineers working in private companies. Once Mr. Khan's business became successful, Abul left his job and then joined the business as regional managers for the entire South Zone. Abul held twenty percent share in the company and were doing quite well for himself. Akash asked if there was any recent stress in the business or personal life but none was evident. Stress in business was usual and grows with growth of the business, so that should not be anything unusual. They did not know of anyone who would have caused harm to their family. Raheel did not add much and mentioned that he has ten percent share to the company and he was still a bachelor with no immediate plans to settle down.

As there was not much juicy information coming through, Akash asked the siblings if they had checked their brother's private office room for any clues but they answered in negative. When he asked the same to Mrs. Haseena, she also answered in negative as she normally did not like going to Mr. Khan's office room which was upstairs. She said, she never appreciated her husband when he was working. As if, it was a dual persona of the same person. He would be so rude, arrogant and business minded when he would be in office. So, she avoided going to that room.

Akash went alone inside the office room. He looked around for anything unusual. He was mainly looking for any kind of notes that could lead to any clues on the place where he last went. He searched for the calendars, diaries and every small sticky notes or any note giving a clue about his whereabouts on the day he went missing. Soon, he found it. Mrs.

Haseena was astonished that it was so simple, if only she knew that her husband writes down his meetings. On his personal study table, clearly written in a small sticky note, '18 Feb 9 pm, A.D Dharamshi'. What does it mean?

Akash was scrutinizing the note as if it was the Terms and Conditions of a Life Insurance. He turned it over and it was all yellow, then he turned it front, it was yellow too, and on it, in Black, the message. What does it mean? he thought 'A.D, what is A.D'? Mrs. Haseena looked at Akash with expectant eyes, thus letting Akash know that the burden of the mystery lies with him to solve. He spent 5 clueless minutes waiting for his mind to slap him a clue about A.D and finally resorted to move on to the next challenge. 'Let's focus on Dharamshi', he said and scratched his head. 'Dharamshi can mean….Dharam!

what does SHI mean then?' 'SHI! SHI! SHI!' he mumbled and shouted 'It must mean nothing related to DHARAM, but then why DHARAMSHI!' Thank god that Akash did not have to continue this misery for too long as soon Mr. Dhole called Mrs. Haseena to inform that her husband's phone tower was last been tracked to Nelamangala region at around 09:30 pm but after that his mobile was switched off. Mr. Dhole was expecting an emotional reaction from the missing person's wife but rather got a very excited one. She triumphantly explained about their findings, as if to prove that she was right in hiring Akash. Initially, Mr. Dhole did not seem any brighter than the two clueless person already involved with the yellow sticky note but as they moved from 'A.D' to the next phase – 'Dharamshi', Mr. Dhole proved to be enlightening. He said that he has often been in Nelamangala area due to his police duties and there is a 'Dharamshi Resort' there. Mrs. Haseena thanked Mr. Dhole and informed of her latest findings to Akash.

'So, if Dharamshi is the destination and 18 Feb is the date of the meeting then 'A.D' means the person he is meeting!' Throughout this sentence, Akash's volume and tone followed a directly proportional curve to time and he was very excited at the end of the statement as he found a sense of achievement in solving this note. 'Do you know anyone whose initials are A.D?' to which Mrs Haseena put a lot of stress to her mind and then answered in the negative. Akash would not take no as an answer 'No one! There must be someone! It is a very common initials, please think again.' Mrs Haseena drummed her right hand fingers in her hair a few times but could not come up with any particular name except few Facebook friends and long distant relatives who should have nothing to do with his husband in the remotest possibilities. Hopeless and helpless, Akash called it a day and asked for his leave and took Mr. Khan's photo with him so that he can ask around Dharamshi Resort.

Next day afternoonish, Mr. Dhole received a call from Akash and Akash urged Mr. Dhole that he needs to come with a search party around Hotel SMS, which is on NH 75, around six kilometers from Nelamangala. 'But why? Why SMS? What have you found?' and Akash just replied that 'It's urgent Mr. Dhole, I am ninety percent sure we will find Mr. Khan here. Please bring a search party. I am waiting here. Please come quickly.' Mr. Dhole though utterly confused and pissed on Akash for not informing him anything properly, had to do something though, based on the urgency in Akash's voice. He managed to arrange for ten men and reached within an hour by when Akash had gobbled up four cigarettes in excitement. He felt he was making a good start to his new specialization of Missing Cases. Mr. Dhole rushed towards Akash like he owed him an explanation but Akash rebuked him by saying that he will explain later and they must search the nearby fields in all directions for Mr. Khan as he fears they don't have much time. Mr Dhole ordered the search and they went in every direction. It was a busy highway, but had a town nearby. With this sudden thrush of excitement of a bunch of police searching their fields, a hefty crowd gathered. Everyone asked the police what they were searching for and the police told the truth 'They did not know'. This encouraged the villagers to start searching too as they were equally placed as the police, they also did not know what they were searching for! Soon the paparazzi joined the party except that they were busy setting up their cameras and interviewing locals and police but no one had any juicy bites for them as no one knew anything and no one knew what they were supposed to know. The search went on for an hour till Akash spotted few stack of hay lying in the field, 50 yards sideways to the highway and under a bill board. One of them had a chunk of flies buzzing around it. Akash called for Mr. Dhole. Everyone including the reporters responded to his call. As Akash started clearing the haystack, a bloody hand moved itself by gravity and soon the awe turned into astonishment as the hand gave way to a blood ripped face, the face of the picture Akash had in his pocket, the face of Mr. Khan.

CHAPTER 5

Among many of the onlookers who had never seen a bloody corpse from this close, Akash was the one who was closest to it and in its first sight, an agony and dis-balance swirled in his stomach. Akash ran sideways, kneeled down and exhaled vomit. He felt very sick but this was not the time for sickness. He had to stay strong and take as much information as he can. The media was relishing the scene and the peanut butter to the bread was Akash, the cheater detective. Breaking News started in every channel and hungry reporters scratched at Akash for an interview but Mr. Dhole shielded him from media. While Mr. Dhole took the bullets of the media over an interview, Akash conjured up the stomach to go close to the bloody scene for inspection along with 2 police inspectors. As they searched the body, Akash found a note and he read it. One camera of the media was focused on him. He scratched his head and looked Up to the advertisement above. When the police inspectors asked him what he was up to, he made a strange face, a face, which a child makes the moment he realizes that he has solved a difficult sum. Just as the child runs to his mother even when mom is busy cooking, to express his excitement for solving the problem and to receive a kiss from his Mom as a reward, Akash ran towards Mr. Dhole who was busy giving the interview to the press and turned him over and said out loud 'I THINK MR. KHAN WAS KILLED BY A SERIAL KILLER!' Each and everyone around said the same word with the same tone at the same time 'WHAT!!!' As Akash tried to explain further, Mr. Dhole put his fingers to Akash's mouth, grabbed him by his neck and took him away from the crowd to an isolated place with no one to eavesdrop or 'mike'drop as the last one was, Akash's last statement was easily relayed through the media mikes and was already being processed for breaking news feeders. Mr. Dhole was about to slap him with rage and even raised his hand but got camera shy. He exploded to Akash but his voice could barely be heard by Akash 'How Dare you tell 'Serial Killer' in front of the media! You Asshole! Now media will go crazy and do you know how much fear this word.... Oh to whom I am talking! Amateurs, I should not have listened to you at all to come here. You just get out from here! Right now!' Akash was taken aback at this shouting at him as Mr. Dhole has always been very nice to him but he did realize what a mistake he has done. He crouched in fear and shame and apologized saying that he could not control his emotion and did not think of the media and he was extremely sorry for it but Mr. Dhole must listen to him why he said so. It was too important for Mr. Dhole not to listen to and so he reluctantly lent his ears to Akash.

'Look at this note' Akash said and handed over a paper, which he had retrieved from Mr. Khan's shirt pocket. It said

'As smokes blaze high and pollute the sky
The river bleeds and only the poor die
I will stand and fight for the future
This businessmen fill their pockets by stabbing Mother Nature
But the law doesn't give a shit
This man's just a start and I will continue to kill it to green it'

Akash then pointed at the billboard below which Mr. Khan's body was found. The billboard aired an ad with an environment friendly message 'Your every small step for a greener surrounding is a big step for BEING HUMAN'. 'This can't be a co-incidence Mr. Dhole, this is too much to be a co-incidence. Mr. Khan was a wood merchant, wood is a source for a Greener planet. There is a serial killer out loose who can cross all limits for a fucking Greener planet. What in the stupidest kind of idiot is he. How can an idiot come to killing for this small a thing? And if he can kill....' Mr. Dhole stopped Akash from saying any further as the media approached them. He took the evidence from Akash and ordered him not to disclose this to any living soul and especially not to Mrs Haseena. He will himself give the news to Mrs Haseena but nothing about the note in his pocket. He also said that this is all bullshit and there is no serial killer running lose. It was just a joke or someone was trying to cover a murder. He again asked Akash not to talk to the media and never give any statement about this letter and as Akash looked quite deranged, he arranged for a car to take Akash home and he again restressed on all the points he just discussed with Akash. Akash nodded and left the scene. He could not dare to call Mrs Haseena and when she called him enroute, he couldn't dare to pick up the phone and switched it off. He was shattered from the inside and the picture of the bloody face of Mr. Khan kept on harassing his mind until sleep called to him for comfort.

CHAPTER 6

Elsewhere, that same day

A crowd always helps. Easier to blend in among the mass and enjoy the mess that one has caused without being suspected. Here, there were reporters, police and locals. Lately, for his own crooked purposes, he always keeps clothes to disguise himself as anyone. He had clothes to disguise himself as rich, poor, lawyer, police, government staff, press and many more. He chose poverty for this occasion and joined the crowd as another villager, covering his face with a nylon cloth. Everyone was looking for something, police, locals and that private detective who has attracted his attention recently. He gave away a sly smile on looking at the media who were covering the search scene. Looking at everyone tirelessly searching for Mr. Khan, he had the urge to join and end the search by pointing out where the body of Mr. Khan lied, but he didn't want any publicity at this point of time and stood back and enjoyed looking at the people all searching in the wrong places. 'Oh, looks like this bunch of rascals would not even be able to find a bed in the bedroom if given a chance.'

At 5ft 8 inch height and with a regular round face, which had rimmed glasses and a small mustache, he was just a common man and it made it so easy to blend in. Enjoying the wreck, he went to a policeman and asked 'What are you looking for Bhaiya!' The police officer rudely pushed him away and said it's none of his business. If only the policeman knew how important he was to this business, he just laughed to himself. He went to few locals and lighted the fire of the rumor that he thinks the police is searching for a dead body. It only took 10 minutes for the fire to light up and burn the media. Soon it was flashing in the TV that the police are searching for a dead body in NH 75. Among all the khaki police officers, the private detective was quite a stand out. His eyes only followed the detective. As if this could be a new challenge to him. He has previously had encounters with police officers, media and goons even and all of them were very interesting but private criminal detectives were a rare species and this one looked yummy to play with. Young and amateur, he can definitely be a turn on. As his eyes followed the detective to the edge of the highway to the stack of hays, his eyes flickered. 'The moment has come!,' He rejoiced. Quietly, he sneaked pass one of the media camera man and pointed the fingers to the detective and said, 'Look, that man is on to something it seems. I think he has found it.' Immediately, the camera followed his fingers and telecasted Akash finding the bloody body of Mr. Khan and Akash embracing the earth to vomit at the site of death. The camera also followed Akash reading a note from the corpse's pocket and immediately rushing to Mr. Dhole. The cameraman swiftly moved his mike to Akash instead of Mr. Dhole and he captured the best bite of the day about a serial killer on the loose.

The 5th 8 inch imposter rejoiced and patted himself at his back. All that was left to disclose was WHY. He could have left this to the capable hands of the media but that would not be satisfying. He went to a local who was curiously standing beside a cameraman, looking at the high end equipment's and admiring them. He went in between then and pulled up the topic of the serial killer on loose. He also said that every serial killer has a motive, which drives them to kill, there is a pattern to follow, and clues left behind. He has seen multiple movies and read about serial killers and all of them are the same. There has to be clues here and the reason must be around. We just need to look at the right places. This got the locals and the cameraman quite excited. Although the cameraman did not show the excitement but kept his right ear open for any findings from the locals about the reason. The local person who was staring at the camera turned out to be quite a prospect for a detective, if only he chose the right career. He immediately surfed the open fields and pointed out that there is nothing here except Hotel SMS at the back and the billboard below which the body was found. Considering that the billboard was much closer to the action, it can have something to do with the Ad in the billboard. The media took the bait as a fish would gobble the worm with a hook screwed through it. The rest was up to the media to spice it up. His work here was done. He happily lighted up a cigarette and went to his car, shoved off poverty and endorsed richer clothes and drove off.

CHAPTER 7

Mrs. Haseena was inconsolable as she shaded her tears in front of her husband's dead body, covered in a white cloth. Her brother in laws looked on without any leak of emotions until the women around gathered by the sobbing wife. Akash initially thought he would skip this sad family demise of the Khans but their family had called and requested him to come as Akash was supportive throughout the case and somehow proved more efficient to the family, compared to the police. The family had lost further trust in police when Mr. Dhole informed them that Mr. Khan's death looked like a hit and run case in the highway by one of the speeding cars but they had to know from the media that he was a victim of a serial killer. When confronted by the family, the police firmly resented the media headlines and said that it was a made up story which fetched more TRP to the media and hence they are projecting it to be so and there was absolute no proof that any kind of serial killer was involved in this mysterious murder. When Akash arrived, he was short of words, for condolences but thankfully, he did not need to say much. Mrs. Haseena was in no position to care about any people around her and the family members just greeted Akash with an appreciating nod, which Akash countered with the same. Mr. Dhole was also present and as Akash went to Mr. Dhole, he did not seem pleased with Akash. He said that Akash has brought a huge media attention to this case by his insincere words in front of media and he is partly to be blamed for all the media harassment that this family has to suffer now.

Talk about the devil. Reporters arrived in their vans outside the residence and started coming in despite the security guard stopping them. It is so hurting to witness reporters stooping down to inhuman moral levels, just for more TRP. Even animals show more compassion than them sometimes. All the flashes and noise of the forthcoming media attention turned everyone's head backwards to the door. Close family members were astonished at the inhuman behavior of the broadcasters but they felt helpless. Distant family members quickly patched their hair to look the best in TV interviews and a joy littered around their face for the 15 seconds of fame. Akash was closest to the door and as he looked at all the family members expression of disbelief for this unwelcome guest, instinct took over him and like a hero he turned towards the news mongers. Their cameras were already on their shoulders and reporters were stretching their hands to make the mike available for a bite. When they were around 15 yards from the main door, Akash smashed the door, locked it from inside, and closed the curtains. He felt good. He turned around and was greeted with smiling responses from everyone except Mrs. Haseena. She only nodded her head in thanks to Akash. Mr. Dhole moved over to the edge of the door to Akash and said 'Now, you will stay in the headlines longer than I thought.'

A door isn't the best obstacle to stop media. They ignored the closed door and began to shout their questions from the other side. The nation wanted to know how people sob at the funeral of a victim of a serial killer and media would not shy away from the duties in delivering that to the people. They kept on shouting from the other side of the door and banging it till it became too noisy an affair. Everyone was taken aback but dare not say anything against the media but it was getting unbearable for Mrs. Haseena. Her sadness was boiling into anger and after 10 minutes of this commotion, she needed to vent. She stood up, dashed her way towards the door and unbolted it and with wet, smudged, fearsome eyes, a grudge and anger in her face that can arouse fear in anyone's heart, she blasted at the reporters for the shamelessness they have been displaying. She was shouting on the top of her voice like a crazy woman. The cameramen took two steps back in her fear but kept the cameras rolling. They knew this was TRP material. Words fumbled in her mouth out of rage and the words that could be made out from her mouth sounded like 'Can't you let me spend my final moments with him in peace? Has the hunger for news shredded you of all humanity…' rest of it was either sobbing or slangs or both. Even with this outburst, reporters completely missed the point and showered her with questions ranging from how is police helping to how she feels at losing her husband to a serial killer. Mrs. Haseena's answer to all of them would have been a further venting of her rage but one question caught her attention and she rigorously cumulated all her anger on that answer and shouted out until a woman in the house pulled her inside and the door was closed again. The question was about her plans to avenge her loss and does she trust the police to avenge on her behalf? She screamed that she has lost all her hopes on the police as they are good for nothing and she throws an open threat to the serial killer that Akash will continue with the case and she has complete trust in the capabilities of Akash and Akash will surely find and kill the serial killer. Its an open challenge from her to the serial killer.

Akash looked stunned as the door closed. He thought the case has closed as per his involvement is concerned. He had taken a 'Missing' case and found Mr. Khan. Case solved. He never agreed to take a murder case and that too, a serial killer! He was trembling. He did not want any money, he was shaking at the thought of going against a serial killer with zero experience with murder cases. Now was not the time to talk to Mrs. Haseena about it and he decided he will shamelessly accept to her later that he is the most unsuitable person for this job. But it was already too late. Although Akash wanted no part in it, to the nation, the game of the serial killer vs Akash Bose had begun and they were pinning all their hopes on Akash to win. Mr. Dhole came to Akash and said 'I told you, itna uro mat, don't fly so high. Now, be ready to fly with the vulture. Also for a note, you have already landed me in quite a mess, so don't come to me again for any help with this issue. If my guess is right and there is no serial killer, 'bach gaye', or else, say Hi to Mr. Khan from my side too.

CHAPTER 8

Elsewhere

He sat in his cozy couch, relishing the chaos caused. A cheeky smile went through his face at the volume of imaginary and made up stories being added by the media to spice it up. He thought 'That's definitely not how it happened but this will keep the audience to their feet and give the important cause, the platform it deserves. Suddenly the TV presenter got very excited about a new development to this case and it showed the private detective that he saw in the field by the highway. The TV channel presented Akash's picture edited with Sherlock Holmes cap. He raised the volume of the TV to lend his ears and saw Akash being presented as the ray of hope against the monster who kills businessmen who pollutes the atmosphere to save the planet. But the monster had a fair bit of sympathy going towards him too, as the people acknowledged and appreciated the cause. People appreciated that at least someone is doing something for the next generations to survive and that, actually, the government is to be blamed for taking no actions, which has driven this person to take up killing as the only option left to save our planet.

He wondered how this private detective has always managed to be on headlines throughout this case. Instead of the murderer and his noble cause, the amateur private detective who did nothing to solve anything gets the people's attention! And few days ago, activists were chanting for the detective's head outside his house. His lips curved a little, thinking about the ping pong that media can do with a character, from a flop to the ray of hope in few moments. He did not expect much challenge from this Akash fellow but he was surprised that police were not taking this case seriously at all. They kept ignoring the clues as hoax. He had expected the police to be on their toes by now but no sign of them anywhere. He has kept his informers on the alert too, to notify him if they see any movement from the police but he has not received any calls from any of his informers. He was just about to close the TV for more important endeavors but got statue-ed. A woman in the TV has thrown an open challenge to the serial killer that Akash will find him soon and kill him. 'Well well well, a challenge huh! then this Akash fellow deserves a visit. You challenged way beyond your league beta, poor fellow!' and he closed the TV to prepare for his next move.

After 2 days, afternoonish, he was in Akash's neighborhood. He had done his homework to know when the detective left his home and returned and when the maid would be alone at home. He dressed himself up with false eye brows and beard and also thick framed glasses which made him look 15 years older than he was. He knew the maid came at 3 pm and left at 4.30. She had a key as Akash would not be at home at that time. Around 4pm, he rang the doorbell in Akash's flat. He specifically chose this hour as the maid would be in a hurry to wrap up her work by 4.30 pm to go home and would not pay him much attention. The maid opened the door and he asked if the detective was available so that he can discuss a case with him. The maid said that he was not at home and would not return before 6 pm. Then, he smoothly said that it's very hot outside and his age does not help either, so he has lost his breath and would be nice if he can sit for five minutes, have a glass of water and then leave. Meanwhile, the maid will also have the time to give the detective's mobile number to him. Considering his age, the maid could not have suspected anything and offered her tea along with water which he gladly accepted as it gave him more time. It was a 1BHK flat and he was sitting in the drawing room. The maid must be one of those 'kaamchors' as the house looked a mess. Everything was spread around, the used plates were in the chair, the glasses in the floor along with unfinished packet of chips. A group of ants made their way to the chips and were having a blast inside the packet. The ants definitely looked healthy and happy with the house owner. He was searching for a spot to keep his spy camera and mike in the drawing room. There wasn't much to hide a spy camera in the room as it hardly had anything decorative. So he only focused on finding a place to keep the mike so that he can listen to whatever the detective would be planning, if he was smart enough to plan anything. Time was running short and he could not find any place, which would keep it out of vision. Finally, the stocks of alcohol bottles on the top shelf caught his attention. Nothing to worry as they were used bottles staggered at a place out of reach, packed at one place to be thrown away together at the end of the year, or two years, may be. A black opaque bottle was his best option and he gathered a chair and stood on it to reach out for the bottle. Just as he got hold of one opaque bottle, which once used to hold elixir, he heard something and turned back to see the maid staring at him with a glass of water in his hand.

It was a very awkward moment, he had a thought of taking aggressive steps about the witness but that would alert the detective, he had to be diplomatic here. He turned towards her and stepped down with the bottle in his hands still. The maid continued to stare at him with disbelief. He laughed and said

'Please do not misunderstand me. Actually I have a daughter who is 21 years old now, studying BBA in Amity University. I had heard of Mr. Bose and heard that he is still a bachelor. I thought if he would be interested in, you know, tying the knot, then.... My girl is quite pretty.... I was just checking the bottles to verify if my would be son in law is a regular drinker. That's all. From what I see above, it does not look to be good news, can you tell me anything about him? Is he dating any girl or is he interested in marriage? Does he have any other kind of bad habits? Does ladies.......come to this flat?'

The maid had enough, she rebuked the questions with an angry look and some regional words. She dropped the glass of water at the sitting table loudly, turned towards the kitchen and on her way in, finally said something understandable, which stated that she is not going to tolerate this type of behavior or answer to any questions. As soon as she went in, he quickly opened the cap, turned on the mike, dropped it inside the bottle, and hurriedly scooted to his seat. The maid came back again to say that there was no milk and she cannot make tea. She clearly did not want to entertain anyone who is looking to bring another lady to the house. Ultimately, everyone looks after his or her job security but her reaction would have been different if she came in to the room again, 10 seconds ago, seeing an old man reaching out for alcohol and sprinting at Bolt speed, back to his seat. But when the maid came back in, he was calmly seated and his mike drop had aroused no suspicion. As per the maid's indirect directive, he left the flat and slowly paced down the stairs to keep on with the act of the old man. Once he was done with the stairs, he ran towards his car, removed all the prosthetics, and dropped a sign of relief. That was a close one. He checked the receiver of the mike and he could hear the maid cursing the old man in the room. So, this shall do fine. He looked at himself in the mirror with a praiseworthy eye and politely patted himself and drove away from the neighborhood.

CHAPTER 9

Since the stint with media at late Mr. Khan's residency, Akash tried to keep a low profile. He did not want to gather attention of any dangerous murderer lurking around in the open. He was not made for this job. His detective career plans were more on the nuptial side, he did not have any wish to investigate anything that involved blood as he cannot keep his stomach straight after witnessing a bloody affair. He thought of lying low for few days till the media tension gets over but reporters were not to let go of him so easily. They were always after Akash to get any kind of interview but Akash always avoided them with media's nemesis word 'No comments!'', Mr. Dhole's anger had slowly subsided as he twice called Akash to ask him if Akash had made any progress. Akash has informed Mr. Dhole that he is not looking into the case and it should be the police's responsibility to look at it. Mr. Dhole only said that police had already come to a conclusion that the letter was just to divert attention from the original murder. Akash knew why Mr. Dhole was so concerned about him. The police inspector was not fully confident, if either the letters were only a hoax but he did not want to engage his force into something premature. So, he rubbished the claims but always kept an eye out on Akash as the detective was most likely to face the wrath of the serial killer if one did exist, as the detective was hyped by the television as the challenger.

Akash himself was very much curious about the serial killer's next steps. He was certain that it was a serial killer and not a hoax. He was constantly at the look out of signs of being followed or he was always waiting for something to happen to him, which will kick of Chapter 2 of the serial killer on loose, but nothing such has happened over the last fortnight but Akash had not let his guards down yet. He always kept Mr. Dhole's number on Speed dial number 1 as he was not sure about his odds against a psychic serial killer. Today also, he had the strange feeling that he was being followed but the millions of times he has looked back, he could not find anyone. By the time Akash reached home, the maid had left. He took a quick shower and lighted a cigarette. As he opened his laptop to catch up with Game of Thrones, his fear came true, Chapter 2 had begun. It was around 11 pm, well beyond office hours but he did not hesitate for a second to speed dial number 1. After eight rings, a tired Mr. Dhole picked up the phone.

Just catching up on a yawn, Mr. Dhole said 'Boliye Akash Babu, what happened?'

'I have received a letter from the killer' panted Akash

'What! What kind of letter? Where did you find it?'

'It's addressed to me and signed by the serial killer who has given himself a name now, The Green man'

'What kind of stupid name is that? Are you sure it's not a prank?'

Akash could not restrict himself from raising his voice 'Enough with your 'pranks'. This is not a prank. Please get serious about it Mr. Dhole. Lives are at stake and all you can think of is prank. Why would a prankster unlock my flat and put a note inside my laptop? Please take it seriously. There is a killer on loose who wants to kill people for a greener planet. Neither is the reason for killing a joke and nor is the threat. You better take it seriously this time, as, if you don't, surely the reporters will treat this letter seriously.'

The tone and the threat put a pause to the telephonic conversation. Mr. Dhole was not too pleased with a threat from an accomplice but all he said was 'What does the letter say?'

'It's a sort of riddle which makes no sense'

'A riddle! Oh my God, this is beyond me. I will come to your house tomorrow morning.'

'Don't you want to listen to the riddle?'

'I only want a good night sleep without any riddles riddling my mind. See you tomorrow at 10 am.' Mr. Dhole dropped the phone and rang up Police Commissioner.

CHAPTER 10

Rajiv had just woken up and had a shower when his daughter, Saloni, came to him with the most difficult problem of her world. 'I just cannot understand Calculus Papa, please help me. I need to complete my Homework.' requested the ninth standard princess. Daughters always consider their dad as a hero but Saloni was spot on to believe that, as Rajiv Mehta was indeed a hero. He was the Superintendent of Police and was one of the best in the Bangalore police force. He held multiple medals for using his sharp mind to trap and catch multiple high profile criminals and had a fantastic resume and most unusual of all, he was honest, sharp and very intelligent. His height of five feet and two inch did not give him much of an upper hand in physical activities and combat and so he relied more on his brains than muscles. Aged at 51, he still carried an innocence in his clean shaved face, a kind of face which gives you a comfort and does not scare you at any angle and does not let you know about his high profile achievements. The most distinct feature about him were his blue eyeballs. It's his eyes only which was his biggest strength as it can find minute details from crime scenes and spot criminal behaviors among suspects.

Just as he had cuddled his daughter and embarked on dealing with Calculus, his phone rang and it was the police commissioner. Rajiv was the go-to man for the police commissioner for all his problems, which needs brain and not a brawl. The commissioner did not make much sense to Rajiv as he was more focused on Calculus then. He only noted down an address where he needed to meet Mr. Dhole about a very serious murder case. Not a single blink at the mention of a murder case, that's how stable Rajiv was. Time, age and experience has taught him to prioritize family at home and worry about work at the police station. Easier said than done but he has successfully trained himself to set priorities as per his surroundings. Leaving the murder issue stranded in his mind, he dived to save his daughter from the hands of Calculus. Mrs. Mehta only smiled at the sight of her two most precious souls solving maths problems. Saloni had approached her yesterday night about Calculus but Maths was Papa's department. With a smile on her face, she served breakfast.

Till Rajiv reached Akash's residence, he did not have any clue what he was getting into. As Mr. Dhole briefed him the case, his eyes became wider. After five minutes of briefing, his first words were 'Wow! Now people have found one more reason to kill - for the planet!!! As if the existing ones were not enough. Now who is this Akash fellow and why is the killer contacting him?' Instead of answering, Mr. Dhole counter questioned 'This case has been in the media for days. Didn't you follow the case in TV, Sir?'

Instead of a straight answer, Rajiv responded, 'Do you want a happy life? Stop watching news channels. Life would be much happier.'

The life coach and Mr. Dhole made their way upstairs to Akash's flat while Mr. Dhole brought Rajiv up to speed with the case at hand.

Chapter 11

As Rajiv made his way to Flat 507, he saw a man in pajamas roaming about the room. 'You must be Mr. Bose, the famous detective!!!' and just as Akash was about to give a shy response to that, Rajiv burst in again, 'I am guilty! As Mr Dhole would like to put me, I am guilty Mr Bose that I am not aware of your fame or your journey to fame, so can you please waste my time and tell me about it.'

Akash thought to himself 'Are all policemen this rude. Leave alone me, this guy is not leaving Mr. Dhole too' but opened his mouth to say 'To not waste your time Sir, let me leave it short and crisp. I am a private detective hired by Mrs. Haseena, wife of the first victim of the serial killer who is roaming about freely out there now and..'

Rajiv broke in again, 'The way you say First victim, seems like you believe there are other victims too! Is there any other victim? Mr. Dhole?'

This time Akash broke in while Mr. Dhole was about to answer 'None yet but if we cannot solve the riddle he has sent me, there will soon be another murder, I am sure of it. Otherwise why would he send the letter to me, that too so much secretively?'

'Exactly my question, why you! Why not the police, why not the CM, why not the fucking media? Why has the letter been sent to you my…My Hero?' Rajiv ended the sentence with sarcasm.

'Because this media has been on my ass all this while and they are just taking revenge, sweet revenge. They portrayed me as the challenger to this serial killer and HE accepted the challenge.'

'Again, WHY YOU? What have you done to the media that they are taking revenge on you? I have been trying to do something to the media for years but could not. Enlighten me, how does one piss off a shameless bunch of reporters'

Akash enlightened Rajiv about the episode of Damini and Shankar.

Rajiv listened. When it was over, he concluded 'OK, so I have to have an affair with a reporter's wife to piss of media! That's why I have never been able to piss them off. If only I had met you before I was married'

Akash sat down on the couch, heaved a sigh and said 'No Sir, you only have to meet with a BITCH. And we did not have any affair, I was cheated.'

Mr. Dhole suddenly laughed and said 'Khaya piya kuch nehi, glass tora bara aana'

'So, how did you get this case? Why did Mrs. Haseena appoint you?' Rajiv restored some order to the discussion with a stern voice modulation.

Mr Dhole knew his short comings can well be exposed if Akash answered this one and hence he interrupted Akash as he was about to answer 'Sir, Mr. Akash was there in the police station when Mrs. Haseena came to register a missing complain about Mr. Khan. Akash already knew a lot about Mr. Khan and so, Mrs. Haseena got impressed with him and hired him to find Mr. Khan.'

Reading Rajiv's looks and anticipating the 'Why.....' coming his way, Akash himself answered that he had done a case study about Mr. Khan in his college days and hence knew about him. Somehow Rajiv found it very hard to accept the co-incidences and asked for Akash to show the case study materials. Akash said that it was a while back and when he moved home, he did not bring it with him as it was obsolete.

'Ok, moving forward, so what did you find in your investigation?'

Again Mr. Dhole sensed danger and answered on Akash's behalf. 'He found a note Sir in Mr. Khan's drawing room.' Then he pumped his chest and said 'Sir, I solved that note and informed Akash about the Dharamshi Resort. I also traced Mr. Khan's last mobile signal to that area, Sir.' A smart grin appeared in Mr. Dhole's face but it wasn't allowed to stay long. Just as Rajiv asked why the police did not investigate the missing person's room and why was a novice detective allowed to take precedence in such a case, the grin packed its bags and made way for the 'sorry' face. 'So we still do not know who was A.D?' Rajiv summarized.

In hope of repainting his image, Mr. Dhole continued with the briefing and informed how he took his force to search for Mr. Khan and how they found Mr. Khan's body and the serial killer's note.

Rajiv totally ruined the painting when we asked Mr Dhole that how he understood that Mr. Khan's body was near Hotel S.M.S. He gave a blank face and said slowly 'Akash……he called me….. and asked to come with a search party as he was sure there was something in the spot!'

Rajiv got furious 'SOMETHING!!! You did not even know what you were searching for and you took your police force with you! On command of a novice detective! Were you going to search or to party! So now you are taking command from general public on how to best use the police's time? This is tremendous irresponsible behavior. You will report to me over a letter why you took your force to that spot. Now just get out of here! Go AWAY!' Mr. Dhole bowed down his head and took his leave.

Akash felt sorry for Mr. Dhole whom he has landed in a lot of trouble. He was about to say something to save Mr. Dhole but could not figure out what to say in his defense but still as he was about to open his mouth to speak, Rajiv turned towards him with a red angry eye and asked 'So, you think you can command the police around is it? This has to stop right now. You are no one, you understand? You are no one to command a police officer on what to do? Do you understand me?'

Akash shaked while he nodded. Rajiv landed his next question with equal anger 'So why did you ask Mr. Dhole to come to Hotel S.M.S.?'

'Next day morning, when I was questioning people around Dharamshi Resort with the picture of Mr. Khan, a shopkeeper said that he has seen Mr. Khan on that night, riding towards the highway. He had stopped for a smoke in his shop and gave a 50 Rupee note for a 15 Rupee Cigarette but did not wait for the change and left. I asked him if he was alone and he answered in affirmative. I opened Google Maps to see what are the possible destination towards the highway and where does it lead to. I saw the Hotel S.M.S in the map and remembered that I had seen the same words 'S.M.S' inscribed in Mr. Khan's diary last page. It did not strike me as anything worth notice then but as I saw the name of the hotel in the map, it looked like a possible destination. When I reached there, I saw Mr. Khan's bike on the road side, left untouched for three nights. That is when I realized that there must be something around here and I called Mr. Dhole.'

Rajiv turned towards the wall in silence, as if he is analyzing the progress so far. He took out a cigarette and sat in a couch. Just as he was about to light up, he paused a bit and looked up to Akash with an enquiring eye and questioned 'Why would Mr. Khan write two destinations to meet the same person? If Hotel S.M.S was his final destination, why write about Dharamshi Resort?'

Akash thought about it and said 'I did not think about it previously but now that you bring it up, maybe he didn't meet one person, maybe he met two different person or maybe he picked up someone from Dharamshi Resort and went towards Hotel S.M.S to meet a third person?'

Rajiv had shut his eyes while Akash was speaking and he said with his eyes closed 'The answer to this 'maybe' can point us to the right direction. You are not as dumb as you look. So, what did the relatives of Mr. Khan behave like, any one as a suspect? I believe they are to be benefited with Mr. Khan's murder, aren't they?'

Akash got irritated and responded 'No I have not thought about that angle but why does none of the policemen want to look at the case from the angle of the serial killer on loose! Why do we keep evading that possibility! I am having letters sent to me from one crazy guy out there and you are still looking at relatives of Mr. Khan!'

Rajiv responded in the smoothest way possible 'Because policemen have seen too much bad in humanity to believe that someone can standup and kill for a noble cause.' He lit up his fag and calmly said, 'Ok, let's see what this guy is sending you. Get me the 1st letter too.'

CHAPTER 12

'The 1st letter is with Mr. Dhole, if he still has it. I will call him.' said Akash.

'No, let me call him, I have been rude to him in the heat of the moment.'

So, Rajiv called Mr. Dhole and quickly apologized for his rude behavior. When Mr. Dhole did come in, he looked much relieved. With his lost prestige redeemed along with the apology, he had a smile on his face for the first time in the day. But when requested for the first letter, his smile was about to disappear again as he did not have it with him and it was at the Police station. He quickly called someone to bring it to him. So, all the attention moved to the new letter that was received.

Akash brought out a printed-paper and laid it in the table.

'In this path of justice, now I have a challenger
So let's give him a fair chance if he can sniff danger
I will have to save the Earth
And kill him before he can give birth
Try and try but you would only fail
The nature's justice will have to prevail'

Rajiv had just finished his cigarette and laid back in the sofa. 'What the fuck does this mean! Where do these psychos come from? Killing for justice! Well the killer would be on the wrong end of justice as he had killed another in the first place, so it's gonna be just a rubbish infinite loop. I don't understand what are these guys thinking before they choose this path. Stupid assholes.'

'Maybe he is doing it because the police and the law are not doing anything' Akash was simple with his reasons to find righteousness in his opponent's actions.

Rajiv got out of his sofa and shouted at Akash 'The police are fighting day and night for justice. We do everything we can to ensure that all criminals are brought under law. Few bad cops example in real life and the misrepresentation of police by Bollywood in reel life makes you assume that we don't work. Do you have any idea what a policeman goes through in his life, not a single public holiday, no family life, not a single day of mental rest, disturbances always in the police station, political pressure, corruption in office, day to day cases of the lowest humanitarian actions possible, rapes, molestation, drugs, murders, terrorism and still we get most of them to law. After all this, our blind legislature lets the criminal go free due to lack of evidence. Do you have any idea how it feels at that point? Knowing that you fought so long to get justice for someone and after all your effort, the criminal goes free! This are all in my normal day to day activities, and what about others who curse the policemen of neglecting their duties, what is their normal source of discomfort in office life! A code not working? Or someone else got a promotion? Do not ever say that a policeman does not do his duties. You have no idea what a policeman goes through.'

Akash was again very polite in putting his next statement 'Your words look more like favoring the actions of the Green Man than against it! Maybe, he is also this much frustrated with the system.'

Before Rajiv could turn back and respond to Akash, Mr. Dhole said 'Mr. Bose, all of us in this room are matured enough to understand what is ethically right and wrong and what is judicially right and wrong. I am sure that all of us are thinking in the same page but we cannot allow these murders to continue, no matter if it is ethically wrong or right. Let's just try to work together and solve this letter everyone.

CHAPTER 13

Elsewhere

He had been quite enjoying his new play toy, a speaker which relays all the conversations in Mr. Bose's personal life. He has recently been very keen about this detective's movements and whereabouts. He has followed him around throughout the day but he expected to be caught or noticed as the one he was following, thinks himself so sharp and agile that he has left a bright career to pursue with such a dodgy profession as a private detective. But he was over expecting from his opponent, Akash did not even get a clue that he was being followed, that his house is bugged and all the conversations they are having at their house with Rajiv and Mr. Dhole is being eves dropped by another. 'Stupid Guy, someone chose the wrong profession' he said to himself and laughed.

After Mr. Dhole has settled the troop to sit and look at the letter, he heard him say 'Lets read out the letter one more time and look for clues here. There must be clues there! Let's look at it closely.' Then Mr. Dhole read out the letter.

'In this path of justice, now I have a challenger
So, let's give him a fair chance if he can sniff danger
I will have to save the Earth
And kill him before he can give birth
Try and try but you would only fail
The nature's justice will have to prevail'

He understood Mr. Dhole to be quite a talkative fellow, as Mr. Dhole still did not stop 'The first line, is there anything there? The path of justice, can that mean anything?'

From the microphone, Akash said 'It can mean the road to Delhi

High court? That's the justice he might be referring too!'

A twinkle came across his eyes.

Rajiv responded 'No, that is one of the most secured places in the country. Of all the places, why would anyone choose that place? It is not strategically correct.'

In his empty room, he appreciated the thought and mockingly clapped

Mr. Dhole said 'So, can it mean any police station? Or the parliament?'

Akash quickly added 'same problem there too, those will be secured places as well.'

Rajiv concluded 'I think we are over thinking about the word 'justice', just like a true policemen. Let's move to the next. May be there is no inner meaning there.'

He could only laugh at the conclusion but kept his ears open for further jokes.

Mr. Dhole read out the second line and said 'There is not much there except the word sniff. Sniffing's more related to dogs rather than human. So, is he calling you a dog Akash babu?'

He again gave away a laughter as he heard Rajiv giving out an irritated sound at Mr. Dhole.

Rajiv urged to move to the third line. Then he read out the third line and confirmed that there cannot be anything there and asked to move to the fourth one.

'This line must point to some clue. You know why?' Mr. Dhole suddenly got into a sarcastic mood and continued his statement 'Because this line is where the murder happens and everyone leaves a clue at a murder.' Mr. Dhole must have put on a proud face after saying it as he thought it to be a very smart observation.

He said to himself in the empty room 'Oh, he is hilarious, I got to meet him. Or maybe he is purely stupid but trying to act smart, yeah that's the case surely.'

Akash was too junior to Mr. Dhole to urge him to shut up but before he could break all the social norms and speak his mind out to Mr. Dhole about his recent joke, he heard a dull, loud thud. Rajiv, in utter frustration, banged his fist strongly on the table as a sign of warning to Mr. Dhole. Mr. Dhole was taken aback and had to literally put his fingers on his lips and gave away a grimace.

To lighten up the mood, Akash said 'Mr. Dhole is right, this line does seem interesting. Among all the other lines, this is the one which most probably points anything out.'

In the empty room, he said to himself 'Yeah, now they are getting somewhere.'

Rajiv looked baffled too and said 'Does not look much, it's quite straight forward to me. What about the next lines? We can come back to this one once we have been through all of them.'

'This 'Try and Try' "Trial and Error" stuff….. doesn't this remind us of a story that we were told in our childhood about a king and a spider!?' asked Akash.

'Yes in that story, eventually there is success and success are not the endgame as per this piece of paper, so we can rule out the spider Mr. Akash' Rajiv must have been thinking what bunch of fools he was dealing with.

The man in the empty room could hardly breathe as he was laughing hysterically, 'Spider!!! King!!! Oh my god I am dealing with a kid here' he said.

Then Rajiv's voice came from the microphone 'Nature's justice? Is he talking about any natural phenomenon like Earthquake, Flood, which are considered as a nature's way to reset?'

'May be, but I still think it's the murder wala line which has clues for us' Akash did not sound interested about any other lines.

Akash continued 'Before he can give birth! Why HE? Shouldn't it be SHE?'

Mr. Dhole's easy-going attitude had an answer for everything 'Arey, Mr. Bose, it's just a proverb, just like my Son's teacher often says to me "You have given birth to a talented child Mr. Dhole, he is a very bright student."'

Rajiv and Akash both sighed and hit their palms hard to their forehead in frustration till Mr. Dhole understood the gesture and resorted to silence.

Akash said again 'I still think it has been intentionally written. Guys do not give birth'

'Unless you are a Sea-Horse' said Rajiv, with a deep thought proceeding that statement.

'Sea-Horse??" exclaimed Akash.

'Yes, male sea horse gives birth to young ones.' Confirmed Rajiv.

The man on the other side of the microphone parted his lips to give away a wicked smile.

'That must mean something, anything, Sea-Horse, Sea-Horse' Akash continued to mumble the same word again and again without any results.

The same word from Akash continued to echo through the microphone.

'…Sea-Horse, Sea-Horse, Samudri Ghora in Bengali, Samudri….. Ghora, Ghora Ghora, oh yes!!'

Suddenly Akash was jumping in his room and shouting 'Yes, Yes, Yes' and punching his fist in the air.

Mr. Dhole and Rajiv became worried and asked 'what happened?'

Akash settled down and said 'Mr. Ashish Ghora, is a famous Bengali industrialist. You must have heard about him in newspapers recently.' Akash looked up expectantly at Rajiv and Mr. Dhole.

Rajiv quickly clarified 'I apologize but I really need to take up the habit of reading newspapers now. Looks like I do not know anything.'

Mr. Dhole said 'Yes I know, he is arrested for polluting River Ganga with his waste plastics.'

Akash answered in affirmative 'Yes, Mr. Ashish Ghora is an industrialist based in my home city, Kolkata. He was charged for polluting River Ganges with plastic byproducts which clogged up one delta of River Ganges and as the water could not flow forward, it flooded a village in the river's bank. Twelve people died due to the flood. That is when he was arrested two years ago and is now out on bail. But his case is still going on in Supreme Court and he is soon to be sentenced.'

Rajiv added 'So, that explains some relevance to the 'Sea' part of Sea-Horse and also the nature's justice as flood. This thoroughly adds up, this is our man. This is the next victim. Fantastic work boys!'

Mr. Dhole chipped in 'I will quickly arrange to call Mr. Ghora and ask him to be careful and arrange for police protection.'

Rajiv ordered 'And get us three tickets to Kolkata, we will have to go and meet him. That gives us a better chance to catch this lunatic.'

The man in the empty room clapped and heaved a sigh of relief. He turned to his laptop to arrange to travel to Kolkata too.

CHAPTER 14

Punishment was nothing new to Ashish Ghora. At the age of twelve, he was rusticated from school for cheating students off their pocket money in return of porn books and CDs. His education was seized since then as he never returned to school again. Being bereaved by his parents at the age of eight, he was brought up in an orphanage, who never cared of his regularity to school. Instead, he opened his own tea stall in front of the school. After few years, when he realized the value of money and was matured enough to understand that his tea stall can never take him close enough to his dreams of being a powerful man, then he secretly started selling alcohol with high markup price to the teens in the locality. Soon, he became popular among young minds from various other areas as well. He shifted his shop to a busier area where he gained acclamation as "Ghora dar Dokan" and it became a 'one stop' for every other school and college punter. His business flourished, he gained fame in the narcotics world and soon, he come in contact with a marijuana kingpin named Munna. He bought marijuana from Munna and secretly popularized it to his business area, which now attracted and included the other ages as well, to his buyers list. As he was new to this affair, he was unaware about the 'paperless' permission he needed to have from the local police by feeding them a good percentage of profit every month for free-flow of such illegal activities. As he had failed to comply with this strict law, the police actioned on it and he was first imprisoned at the age of 23.

Even jail turned out to be a boon to him as for the first time he was in a place where he can make some serious contacts. He became friends with multiple cheats, criminals and murderers and most importantly, he managed to have acquaintance to some corrupt police officers. Once he was released, the door for downfall was wide open and Ashish made the most of it. He started a racket of marijuana, drugs and Bengal's local liquor. With all his new contacts, his bribed police constables would warn him beforehand if there was a plan for a police raid at his factory, his criminal friends would be summoned for handling any local disturbance and his prison mates, who were now settled in other cities, helped him to spread his business across multiple other cities in India. With more power and money, Ashish attracted rivalry and life threats from multiple other drug lords but his main rival had always been Mr. Debasis Sen, who handed a drug racket in Kolkata. Debasis was not as sharp as Ashish but envied Ashish's growth so much that he even tried to get Ashish killed by goons but Ashish came out unharmed.

Within ten years, his business had expanded to fourteen cities in India but soon, tragedy struck him. He got approached by locals to be an MLA for the ruling party. A step, which he thought to be a step up the ladder in his dark career, took away all the other steps, which were below. The opposition party knew about his claim to fame and used it to their best advantage. Media pounced on him like a dog and exposed all his criminal businesses. With the pressure of the party mounting up, he had to close operations of most of his unlawful businesses overnight but the fire had already been lit in the forest. Although he had closed operations of his illegal businesses, the reporters had gathered enough proof and ran it as a local breaking news. He also had his own enemies in this wicked line of business. As soon as they saw him to be weak and righteous due to the media pressure, they attacked his men and factory and took over them one by one. He couldn't himself do anything about it in fear of the media but asked his right hand, Bikram Pal to fight back but he too betrayed him and swayed all his men and joined his rival, Debasis Sen. These were illegal affairs which does not require any paper-work, the throne belongs to whoever has power. Within a fortnight, he was deprived of everything, he had no business, no goons, no social status, but what he only had was lots of enemies. Finally, he was a corruption free MLA, all the corruptions were in his past now. But the opposition were still campaigning against him and the ruling party feared that they were losing crucial votes. As a mother of irony, as soon as he became corruption free, the ruling party expelled him from his post of MLA on corruption charges. As an offline settlement, as he had lost everything for the party, the party gave him a factory, which made plastics from raw materials so that he can at least earn a living out of it.

His life had changed 180 degrees now. A thought crept on him that as he is starting a new life, why not take few 360 degree turns now, seven to be exact, around a fire, with a lady, the lady who would be the lady of his life. Few days of search, rather, let's put it as few months of search and there you go. Ashish found himself taking his dreamy 360 turns around the fire along with Mrs. Sudeshna and thus, the Ashish of College Street became Mr. Ashish Ghora, former MLA and proprietor of Ghora Plastics Private Limited. Things went the honest way for the next 15 years and they had two son too but one day, his past came knocking at the door. As he opened his office cabin, he saw his traitor, Bikram Pal, standing and smiling at him. In an urge of rage, he caught hold of his arms and twisted it to his back and locked Bikram to a surrendering position. Bikram was grasping for breath but still managed to say, that, he feels guilty every day to have betrayed Ashish and Ashish has every right to hit him with all he can but today he came as a friend to discuss business. He said that he knew that Ashish's business was not doing too well and it can never satisfy Ashish's dreams. He also said that he has a business proposal to turn both of their fortunes. But Ashish still could not come to terms with Bikram but his fighting days were well over. He did not have the mentality anymore to torture someone but he found a slight exception in this case, he took his burning cigarette to his hand, and snubbed the burning end to the locked left forearm of Bikram. Bikram screeched in pain and then Ashish released him. Bikram looked at the wound and accepted the burning sensation as the punishment, smiled back and said 'So, can we discuss business now?'

Bikram had a client which wanted to make an illegal chemical but it needed a factory and a lot of bio waste would be created of it, hence Bikram had reached out to Ashish as he was the only one he knew who held the infrastructure and a license to dispose waste into the River.

Although his license never allowed for what he was proposing but it would provide some cover at least. In return, he proposed a 40% share to Ashish. Ashish's financial condition and his luxurious dreams meant he had no choice but to accept it, knowing well enough what he was taking on. As this pseudo business started, Ashish became richer by each day. He got himself a great bungalow, high-end cars and foreign trips for his family. As long as the luxury was coming through, the family never questioned where it was coming from. But Ashish's waste disposal was touching sky limits. He further bribed police officers and environmentalists to keep the hype as low as possible, but a few years along, it started to rain heavily during the monsoons. It rained continuously for three days. Near his factory, a village by the bank of the river flooded and multiple people died. Now, once the worst was already done, the media and the political pressure mounted on the police. Environmentalist claimed that the village could not have been flooded as the banks were high enough and could have tolerated three more days of rain. Upon investigation, it was found that Ashish's factory was dumping excessive waste to the river Ganges. The type of waste he does not have license for, the type of waste which damages water quality and kills fishes and humans who use the water and this waste had blocked all the nearby pipelines in the river and hence the level of water rose and it got flooded. Ashish was arrested again and this time too, the media pounced on him. Although he was out on bail but this case against him has been going on for two years now and the final verdict was due on next month.

CHAPTER 15

As Akash and Rajiv landed in Kolkata, they went to the Bidhan nagar police station, which was handling Mr. Ghora's legal case. There they met with Mr. Chanchal Paik, who was the investigating officer for this case. Mr. Paik briefed them in details about Mr. Ghora's childhood until he was arrested and later released on bail. Akash asked 'The court verdict next month, what seems to be the likely sentence?' to which Mr. Paik confirmed with full confidence that it's an open and shut case and he will surely get imprisonment for life. He also believed that even Mr. Ghora and his lawyer knows about it and hence Mr. Ghora has been holidaying a lot lately, knowing fully well that this are his last days of freedom. Mr. Paik was also curious about the curiosity of Rajiv and Akash regarding Mr. Ghora and hence Mr. Paik had to be briefed about the 'Green Man'. Mr. Paik looked spell bound after hearing it, he said 'Bolen ki Moshai! Serial killer! Tao abar for the environment? Instead of businessmen, if we could brainwash him to divert his attention towards some criminals, he could have been our Turup ka iqqa, jakey bole, Ace of spades.' Akash quickly added 'Criminals can kill only few but these businessmen are killing the total future of next generations, bujhlen Paik babu? This businessmen are more dangerous to our future than criminals.' Why would Rajiv stay quiet, he said 'Looks like the Green man has gathered quite a fan following. What he is doing is wrong and it is our duty to bring him to justice. If his fans cannot shoot him, I will.' He left the company of the two for a smoke outside the police station, he definitely wasn't pleased with both of them. Akash said to himself, loud enough for Mr. Paik to be an audience 'If it comes to shooting, I am dropping the gun and running away. I have never touched a gun in my life.' Mr. Paik responded 'But if you drop the gun, will the Green man drop it too, or will he drop you?' Akash realized that he was already deep in this mess. He just hoped he had a better life insurance.

The team boarded a police jeep and directed themselves toward Newtown where Mr. Ghora owned a bungalow. As they reached, Rajiv could not help but appreciate the beauty of the bungalow. It was thoroughly maintained and they even had a gardener ploughing the field. Akash asked the gardener if Mr. Ghora was available to which the gardener replied in the negative and so Mr. Paik ordered the gardener to inform Mrs. Sudeshna that the police wanted to see her. The gardener touched Mr. Paik's feet and said 'Jo hokum', left to call Mrs. Sudeshna. They waited outside for five minutes but still, no one showed up, so they themselves went inside the house.

Police was nothing new to Mrs. Sudeshna as she has been dealing with them for quite some time now since her husband's latest doom. Akash literally checked her out when she approached them. Akash had not yet grabbed that subtleness of his idol Sherlock Holmes to look and understand every small details about a character in just one simple look but he never stopped trying to reach that level. The outcome-an uncomfortable stare and checking out of the person opposite, although Akash has never yet been able to deduce anything from their looks. All good things start at their own good time and looks like, the good times were here. For the first time, Akash was able to take away a few pointers from checking out the lady opposite to her. She had a politeness about her that can calm any beast down with the beauty of her face. She was 45ish but nothing could hide that she had once been a very beautiful woman. No wonder Mr. Ghora left his negative past for her. Her eyes were upturned, like a cat's and her nose was perky, this two distinct features about her made her appealing. A part of the cheeks, closer to the left eye was having over make-up to hide something, some wound marks may be. As Akash's stare moved downwards, he noticed a reddish spot along both her forearms, like someone had gripped her tightly by the arms during a recent quarrel. Akash could not complete his stare any further down as everyone in the room was staring at Akash who was busy doing the stare and finally Mr. Paik put a full stop to it by patting Akash's shoulders and saying out loud,

'Rajiv Sir, please arrange to get him married soon.' Akash felt so ashamed that he knew he was out of the game of questioning and just took a seat in the sofa. Rajiv broke the silence and said, 'Your gardener said that Mr. Ashish Ghora is not at home, can you please tell us where can we catch up with him?'

Mrs. Sudesha sounded surprised 'Gardener? We do not have any gardener in this bungalow!'

As all of them got alerted at the same time and said 'What!!' Rajiv made a run for the doorway but the garden was empty. 'Shit! Did anyone see his face?' Rajiv knew that a positive answer was unlikely and he was right. No one notices how a gardener looks like but what was he doing here worried Rajiv more?

'What was he up to?' said Akash

'Surveillance' responded Mr. Paik and quickly kneeled down to his feet and pulled out a small disc shaped object from his shoes, in the size of a shirt button.

'Mike, that's what he added to my feet when he knelled down, so that he can listen to our conversation.'

Rajiv took the button shaped mike, shouted 'Fuck You, Green Man!' and stubbed the mike in his feet.

As the tension calmed down, Rajiv saw that Mrs. Sudeshna was trembling in fear as to what is happening to her world suddenly. Rajiv knew to what extent a wife can worry about her husband if she would come to know that her husband is now a target of a serial killer and so he said 'It's the media Madam! They are trying all their tricks to get some news before next month's final verdict about your husband's case. We are from Police and we are here also about the case, so that we can submit our final charge sheet.'

Regaining her calmness, she replied 'Tell me officer, how I can help you.'

'So, where is your husband now?'

'He is gone to meet our family Jyotish, Baba Sachdev'

'I see you have three fortune stones in your fingers, does everyone in your family believe in astrology?'

'Lately, our family has been going through some turmoil and so, we have left our fate to God and astrology has helped us a lot to redeem our luck. Initially, my husband did not have any interest in it but I persuaded him to consult with Baba Sachdev and since then, he has seen genuine improvements by wearing the stones and he is the most firm believer now in our family. Even my kids believe in astrology. I can tell you of so many instances where Baba Sachdev predicted the future correctly.'

Mrs. Sudeshna would not have stopped if Mr. Paik had not interfered 'When will he be back, we need to talk to him about the case.'

'He should be back by midnight as Baba's house is quite far from here.'

'Ok, so we shall come to meet with him tomorrow'

'How old are your children Mrs. Sudeshna?' Rajiv continued the questions although Mr. Paik did not find any relevance or need for it.

'Shiv is twelve and Anju is ten years old.'

'Are you a housewife or are you working?'

'I am a housewife only, with two kids, it's very hard to find time for myself, leave alone time to get myself a job.'

'Please do not mind my question, but what if, your husband is given a life sentence next month? What are your financial plans for the family?'

'No, there's nothing to mind, rather, I thank you for your concern about it. We have discussed this during the length of time. Ashish has already transferred everything he owns to my name including this house. If it comes to it, we will sell this house and move to my mother's house. I will also get some support there. Apart from that we have few jewelries, three FDs and Ashish has also raised the premium of his life insurance by quite a lot recently to support us if anything happens to him.'

She paused and then continued 'He is a good husband you know, he loves me a lot, he loves his family and he is a good person. He just dreams of more time to live with us, that is all he wants, please help us' and she broke down.

It's very uneasy when a lady breaks down to crying and there is nothing you can say to console her. Mr. Paik only said that the Police is here to help them if they need anything and he will also post a guard outside the house so that the media does not disturb again. He also asked to inform Mr. Ghora to come and meet him at 11 am tomorrow morning at Bidhan Nagar police station and they took her leave, leaving a petite woman, crying off her grief.

Chapter 16

First call went unanswered, so did the second. It was the third call that Akash picked up. He was in deep sleep. He coud not even open his eyes to check who was calling but just answered it with a nappy Hello. It was Mr. Paik on the other side of the phone and he sounded very alarmed and excited. With his sleepy eyes, Akash could not make most of it and so he got up, turned on the bedside lamp and looked at the clock. It was 2 am in the morning. He swiped his eyes with one hand and asked Mr. Paik to repeat the words. 'The Green Man has killed his second victim, it is indeed Mr. Ghora. He met with a car accident in the Kolkata-Digha highway at around midnight.'

Akash jumped back to his sense and shouted 'What!! Oh No, how did it happen, where did it happen?'

'Get ready, I am calling Rajiv and then I will pick you up in 30 minutes. We need to go to the spot right away.'

'Rajiv is in my hotel only, please pick us up from Park Hotel. I will wake him up.'

Rajiv picked up on the second ring and was equally shocked to hear about the sudden demise. After 30 minutes, both of them were down at the lobby, waiting for Mr. Paik. There was an awkward silence between them and the annoying clock ticks only made the silence more noticeable. A thought of fear gushed through Akash's vein. He was dealing with a cold-blooded murderer here. The accident cannot be a co-incidence, surely not. He quickly dressed with a trembling heart and met Rajiv in the lobby. Mr. Paik was a man of his words as he arrived exactly on time. He looked so normal. He even greeted them with a joke 'So, you two troublemakers are partying together and did not bother to invite me! Why invite the grumpy police officer?' Rajiv shared a smile and said 'Welcome to the After Party Mr. Paik.' Mr. Paik smiled back and said 'Hope you party animals had some good sleep!' Akash still could not make out how this two insensitive person were exchanging jokes when someone is dead and so he preferred to be a listener only. This did not stop Rajiv though. 'We had some food and drinks till 11 and went to our rooms for some sleep till you crashed in with this news.' Mr. Paik gestured to go to the police jeep as he said 'You can have some time to catch up on your sleep as the accident site is two hours away from here.' Akash could not help but feel pleased from the last statement and all three of them made good use of the long journey to the accident spot. It was like a snoring competition and occasionally the car horn joining in the band to deliver a symphony.

The accident spot was about three kilometers from Mecheda, which was the nearest decent Railway station on the highway. As they approached the accident site, they saw layers of smoke thickened the air and was sourced from a flipped and completely damaged car stranded at the roadside. Mr. Paik asked one of the officers to brief the situation. The policeman said 'The car was going towards the city when the driver, Mr. Ghora, suddenly lost control and flipped 180 degrees and went off the road. The car engine caught fire while Mr. Ghora was knocked unconscious by the impact. It was past midnight and this is an empty stretch of land. There were no villagers here. The sight of the burning car caught attention of few passer by drivers and they called us in. Before we could reach the site, there was a blast due to the fuel tank igniting which left the chances of Mr. Ghora surviving by a thread. The fire brigade came and did its job but it was too late. When we brought out the body, there was no skin left in the body, it was all burnt. We identified Mr. Ghora by the car registration number and informed the family members and the Lal Bazaar Police station.'

Chapter 17

At the accident site:

The locals had gathered near the accident site, which gave him a good alibi to bring on his rugged shirt and lungi and mix with the crowd. He could not afford to be too close to the police officer and the detective as they had seen his face in Mr. Ghora's residence. Though they have only seen him in disguise but it was too stupid a move to go much closer to encourage the possibilities of getting identified. So, he stood back, enough to still hear what the detective was discussing with the police officer. He heard Rajiv say 'When did this happen exactly? To which the police officer responded a time close to midnight. Rajiv then again continued 'How do you know that this is Mr. Ghora?' The police officer looked to have found some kind of fun in this question. 'As I said, we refereed to the car registration number and also, Mr. Ghora is infamous in this city. Everyone knows him. We had verified with the nearest toll station and they had seen Mr. Ghora in this car at around 11.30 pm. Also, the age and the build matches the body. There are some documents too which were retrieved, half burnt. You can take a look at it if you want to.'

Rajiv continued 'Yeah we will look at that and the body but before that, was there anyone else in the car with him?'

The police officer nodded his head in denial and said that the Toll officer saw him alone.

'Where is this toll station?'

The police officer said '10 kilometers away.'

'I need CCTV footage of the toll station to confirm if the man driving this car was Mr. Ghora.'

'Ok as you don't believe me, I will arrange for it but why is it necessary Sir, why do you doubt that this is Mr. Ghora? All of us know about this man and we are sure that it was him.'

'That's the problem, you do not know anything about this case. Just provide the details that Rajiv Sir is asking for and show us the burned docs.' Commanded Mr. Paik who looked to have the final say in the discussion.

The man in the poor apparel gave a cunning smile and repeated 'Yeah, he does not have any clue about the real case, indeed he doesn't.'

All of them went to look at whatever documents had been retrieved but there was not much to go by.

Most of it were burnt. There was few legal documents but not much to give a lead.

The man turned his attention to Akash when Akash went near the burned body. Same result. Akash had one close look at the burnt body and quickly stepped aside to vomit. The man quietly laughed to himself and mocked off the word 'Challenger!!!!'

Soon the media made their way to the accident site and setup their interview camps, Mr. Ghora's family members also arrived and the whole scene turned dramatic with sounds of grief hovering in the air. 'Look like it's a wrap.' He concluded and left the site.

CHAPTER 18

In Mr. Paik's police station, Rajiv was seating silently, staring at the abyss while Akash was roaming around and cursing 'Why! Why! Why! How could we not stop him? We got the clue right and we were so close to save him, but we failed. Even if we could have informed him over phone about incumbent danger, maybe we could have avoided a death.'

Rajiv added from his seat 'May be, we could have avoided loosing and won against this maniac.'

Akash was stunned and responded 'You seem to value winning more than the life of this man Rajiv Sir.'

Rajiv blankly responded 'Your 'this man' valued money more than the lives of so many villagers. If you were in my shoes for the length I have been, your heart would not even melt if Mother Teresa died, leave alone a criminal's death. We have seen too much disturbing scenes to worry about the death of a murderer. What I still can't get my head around is 'Why!''

Mr. Paik was not someone to stay quite when two other men are talking and so he questioned in his mother tongue ' 'Why' nia ki problem?'

Rajiv continued 'If you are a serial killer out to do the right thing for the nature, why would you kill someone who is supposed to be jailed for life anyways, in a month's time! Mr. Paik, you said for sure that he was going to be jailed, right?'

Mr. Paik did not realize that he would be taken on his words and so he tried to correct it and say 'Well, it's not that much certain but that is what the rumour is, the case did not sway to Mr. Ghora's direction. But you never know with the law, so cannot confirm, but it surely looked like it.'

Akash said 'May be he does not believe in the law? May be that can reveal us something about his identity? Which sort of people does not believe in the law?'

Rajiv spoke out 'He does not believe in the law but he is killing for Justice! That sounds absurd. Also, no one in India believes in the law, this does not rule anybody out of suspicion. We have to find another approach but I can't help but feel that he chose Mr. Ghora for a reason, which will point us to him.'

Akash added 'Does anyone remember the gardener's face? May be that was the Green Man!'

Mr. Paik said 'I do not remember the face but I can surely recognize it if I see him again. Also, he must have been in disguise if it was him but he did not look like a killer.'

Rajiv said 'What are you expecting Mr. Paik, a muscular man with a machete in his hands or a gun tucked in his belts? We are dealing with a common man here, a smart common man with a passion for riddles and hell bent on taking actions to save the future. May be he has lost someone to a natural devastation like flood which is causing this anger in him.'

Akash looked to be having a second thought for the last few seconds and he finally spoke 'What is the difference between a common man and a professional criminal? Common man are not that twisted and they are more prone to error in the murder site than the criminal.'

Rajiv said 'Mr. Dhole said that he had investigated thoroughly in the first murder site but did not find any substantial clues. Mr. Paik also searched for clues when the crowd cleared, but there were none. Are we dealing with a professional here?'

Suddenly a light bulb flashed on top of Akash's head 'Crowd! You said crowd?'

Rajiv looked ridiculed 'Yeah but what's funny in that?'

Akash continued 'Crowds are formed of common men and why do crowd's form? Because they are curious and always on the lookout of something different from there monotonous life. If Green Man is indeed a common man, he would definitely be curious and would not be able to resist the temptation to see his own work unfold successfully. He would surely be present in both the murder sites and as they are two different cities, we should not usually have a common face.'

Rajiv suddenly got excited 'Great point Dude, you are indeed the challenger. Mr. Paik, please arrange for all media footage, uncut, from both the sites and check for a common face. Please act on it immediately. Now we are going to nab him. May be a face will remind us of the gardener too, so we have 3 references to go by, fantastic, let's wait for this investigation to come out.'

CHAPTER 19

Next morning, Akash quickly caught up with Rajiv in their hotel during breakfast to check if they have any update on the validation of video footages. Rajiv laughed and said, 'Patience brother, its police force, not the Avengers, this kind of things take some time. They have collected the footages yesterday night. From today, the officers will search for a common face in between the videos. I have asked to text me even small updates, if any. That way, we can be on top of the findings. I know why you are so anxious but this needs time.'

'But by then, he will move on to the next victim and another life will be at risk. Every second counts.'

Rajiv responded 'Yes, but the timer does not start until you get another letter.'

'What does that mean?'

'Serial killers have a trend, they have rules and they cannot go beyond that rule. You are now in his game. He will have to give you a chance to stop him. He just cannot go about killing people anymore. He has to send you a note, give you a fair chance to catch him and then try to kill his next victim. That's the rule he has set and that is how the game will be played. So, until we receive the next letter, the timer does not start.'

'All of this is a game! A man's life is a game?'

'Don't lecture me, I can vouch that I am not your Green Man. Save the lecture for your Green Man if you can ever catch him.'

'Me! Catch him! I thought it was your job! I am fucking scared Rajiv, I am up against a killer with no idea what I need to do. I don't even know what I would do if we comes in front of me. I will not be able to do anything and he will surely shoot me. Why the fuck did I get into all of this? Rajiv, please help me, I do not want to die, I just want a peaceful life. Please help me.'

'Peaceful! Then why did you leave your job, which peaceful man decides to be a private detective? Don't worry, you are no industrialist, so you cannot be on his list and you are his challenger, you are his sweet devil, he cannot live without you anymore, so whatever happens, you two have a bond now and he cannot kill you, that is another rule.'

'How do you know so much Rajiv?'

'Bollywood.' Rajiv laughed and continued 'On a serious note, I was the sidekick for Delhi ACP, Rishi Gujral when he was involved in the Delhi Serial knife stabs 7 years back. We had to study 'The Stabber' for 14 months until we caught him at his 13th crime scene. I guess 13 was unlucky for him.'

'What kind of a name is Stabber?'

'Well we had to give some name; he did not exactly leave his business card you know. Thankfully, Green Man named himself. Otherwise, we would have searched for names, which sounds spooky. Trust me, its not an easy job, naming someone.'

Akash had the last laugh when he said 'Something tells me you were not allowed to have anything to do with naming your daughter.'

Rajiv just became grumpy and said 'Very funny, but yeah, all my suggestions were thrown down the bin. I wanted to name her Shanti'

Akash could not stop laughing and Rajiv could not figure out why he was laughing. Akash finally controlled himself, said, 'That's my maid's name', and again burst out laughing.

When he finished laughing, Akash asked 'So, how did you catch the Stabber?'

'We cracked down the clues and got to the murder site before him and waited for him to come. He somehow knew that we would come but he had no choice, he had to go along with his game. He did try to quickly stab the victim and make a run for it; his usual style was to torcher for hours. We had surrounded him from all sides, when he saw that he had no routes to escape, he gave a sick laugh at us and slashed his wrists without a second thought. That laugh haunts me till date. That was one mother fucker mad man. I hope Green Man is more on the gentle side.'

Akash concluded 'Let's hope that number 3 is unlucky for Green Man. By 13, I will die out of tension.'

Both finished their breakfast and went to their individual rooms but shortly, Rajiv received a call from Akash.

'The timer has started, Come to my room immediately.'

CHAPTER 20

Rajiv turned up immediately and Mr. Paik followed in a few hours. He had brought one of his bright colleague too, Mr. Ghosh, whom he described was his 'Problem Solver'. Anything the issue, Mr. Ghosh can solve it. A very handy person to have in this kind of situation where all they need is to break this riddle.

You failed!! Ha Ha!! but do not give up the fight
When time stands still, the brightest night
Must sacrifice in its hardest hair
Ware he to win the dragon's lair.

Only dead silence prolonged for the next 30 minutes with frequent sound of the nails scratching the hair (for those who had it, as Mr. Ghosh was scratching his bald head). Turn by turn, all of them would take the paper, read it thoroughly again and again, mumbling all the lines and would often show a sign of being hit with the arrow of intelligence as they would get up from the seat in excitement, but then again, as if the same arrow has hit their heart, they would sink down on the sofa. Rajiv took to his pill of smoke to unwind his intelligence. Mr. Ghosh was the first one to speak out after all this prolonged silence. 'Brightest Night, that makes sense as the full moon night, when is that? That should be the day the Green man would strike.'

Mr. Paik said 'Purnima raatri te? The night of the full moon? Did anyone look at the moon yesterday, what was it's size?'

None of them was romantic enough to admire the moon at least once every night and so everyone agreed to denial. Mr. Paik resorted to dial the one person, who he could trust with information's on the lunar cycle. 'Hello, listen, when is Purnima? When will you do the Puja for the full moon?'

His wife had her own questions before she would enlighten Mr. Paik. Akash could hear Mr. Paik say

'Arey I will have my tiffin later on and everything is fine, please just tell me, when is Purnima

puja?....Tonight! .....Are you sure? Ok I will call you later on..... Haan ami tiffin kheye nebo, rakhlam.'

As he disconnected the call, he confirmed that tonight is the night of the full moon. So, it's going to happen tonight. Now they needed to know When, Where and Whom does it concern.

Mr. Paik continued 'Do not give up the fight reminds me of Rocky Balboa? How about you guys?'

Akash gently said 'The word can refer to many movies or incidents, it is difficult to pin point. 'Hardest Hair' and 'Dragon's Lair' that is what my mind is tingling on. Dragon's lair is the home of the princess in the magical stories, so can it have anything to do with that?'

Rajiv put his opinion forward 'Possible, but a princess is not a 'murdery' thing actually! May be it is a clue but I am not able to dig on it. I want to go step by step, we have the date, let's focus on the time if we have the information here. 'When time stands still' That is where the 'time' is mentioned, I am just sure of it.'

Akash did not add any value by asking the obvious but he did not back out from asking 'So, when does time stand still?'

Mr. Ghosh listed all the options 'Here is what I think, New Year at 00:00 midnight? When someone dies or has a heart attack or maybe he meant the time when your clock's battery dies out!'

Mr. Paik seemed quite a ladies man when he said 'Or maybe he means the time when you are in love and you are looking at your lover's face with passion and....'

Rajiv stopped Mr. Paik in his love tracks and said 'Thank you Paik babu but I think Green man does not want us to stare at a girl's face right now, I think Ghosh babu has a point with the heart stopping or someone dying part, that is more relevant to the case. But how can we point out a single time from that. This is shit yaar, Akash, what do you think?'

Akash looked quite busy with himself and he replied 'I am more fascinated with the battery dying out example.'

Mr. Paik again spoke up 'But battery of a clock can die at any time, how do you get a fixed time from that?'

Akash looked sideways towards the wall clock when he said 'But what if we refer to the time the battery starts its life, what is the time from which every clock starts its life? If you go to any clock shop, you will see all the clocks mounted all around you, all pointing to 10:10, every new clock has the same time set till you put on a battery, so that is the time when the clock stands still, I mean 'time stands still''

Everyone came up to Akash and patted his back vigorously and Rajiv complemented him 'Master stroke, looks like you truly are thinking like the Green Man now.'

Mr. Paik did the conclusions, 'So, we have the time, let's look out for Where and Who'

'Hardest hair! Can we google that one and see the results' suggested Mr. Ghosh - the problem solver referring to everyone's problem solver – www.google.com

All four of them searched the same phrase over and over again till Akash said 'Here is one weird fact, the Rhino's horn is actually compacted Hair. The composition of the Rhino's horn is actually that of hair! This can be what is meant by the hardest hair, what say?'

'Rhino horn!' Exclaimed Rajiv. 'What can a Rhino have to do with our person or place? Is he gonna kill a tribal in a jungle?'

'Kaziranga National Park is famous for Rhinos, maybe the place is Kaziranga!' confirmed the bald problem solver.

'A forest or a national park should not house any business man, unless he means to kill someone who is on vacation to a National Park. Or maybe he is referring to any business man, whose actions killed a lot of animals in a national park!' Added Mr. Paik.

'Well, I do not know of any such man but we are getting too diverted, the possibilities could be vast or maybe he did not mean Rhinos.' said Akash.

'So, what do we do then?' The problem solver raised the problem.

'Let's work on the other pieces and may be this will settle in finally.' Wisely suggested by Rajiv.

Rajiv quickly observed 'The last lines of the letter, why does it say 'Ware' instead of 'Were'?'

Mr. Ghosh said 'It must be a clue; the word 'Ware' does not individually hold any meaning that I am aware of.'

Mr. Paik commented 'By 'Ware', the only thing that comes to my mind is a Warehouse; nothing else really starts with this word.'

Akash observed 'Funny thing, 'Dragon's lair', 'lair' in some senses does mean 'House', so if you combine those two, 'WareHouse' does make a lot of sense.'

Rajiv brought back the problems on the table again 'So, what does Dragon and Rhino, or the hardest hair actually mean, Why Dragon? Why not Lion, Tiger or a Cow for god's sake'

Akash could not control his giggle as it spat out as a laughter 'Cow's lair, that would be something to watch for' Everyone could not follow up on their serious face anymore by Akash's comment and burst out laughing.

Everyone laughed except the problem solver, who was still drumming his bald head as he looked at the window, thinking, as if, he is sharpening his mind with the drumming 'Now that you say 'Warehouse' and 'Rhino', you know, we do have a Rhino Warehouse in China Town but it's long been closed off.'

Akash jumped up at hearing this, 'Rhino Warehouse, China Town, That explains the Dragon, The hardest hair, the 'Ware' and the 'Lair'. I think, this is it. It matches with everything. I am sure it is Rhino Warehouse, China Town. He said 'Must Sacrifice IN it's hardest hair' Akash stressed a lot on the 'IN'. 'That 'IN' makes it a weird sentence but it can make sense that the sacrifice will be inside the Rhino Warehouse!'

Everyone got up on their feet and agreed in excitement.

'Well done everyone. So, we have the where and when, let's check who he has targeted to kill.' Congratulated Rajiv.

'The letter's already over, there is no mention of 'Who'!' Mr. Paik stated the fact.

'The 'Who' has to be here, we need to look at it again.' Commanded Rajiv.

'May be he did not mention the 'Who' as there are no further lines.' Said Akash.

But Rajiv was adamant, 'No, No, it cannot be. A serial killer has to follow a pattern. It's his rules and even he cannot break it. The previous letter had the 'Who', so this letter has to have the same. He cannot break his own rules.'

'But the previous letter did not have the 'When' and 'Where'. This one has that.' Said Akash.

'But, but, that's not how the psyche of a psychic serial killer works.' Justified Rajiv.

'May be he isn't a psyche, just a normal man, at least that's what this letters point out, he is mentally disturbed or lunatic in some sort but not completely psychic.' Said Mr. Ghosh.

'Its already 7 pm, we got to go to the Warehouse quickly and before that, we need the building plan for the Warehouse so that we can strategize, otherwise, we will be one step behind the Green Man again as he must have already plotted everything and even his escape route. Otherwise, he would not be confident enough to give us the time and place. I will arrange for the building plans, you guys do the planning to stop him. I will be back by 8.30 pm with my force. We need to be there by 9.30 pm' Mr. Paik took the lead and was about to leave the room.

Akash quickly added 'Do not bring an army, that way he will be alarmed, he must be scouting the place before he goes for the kill, so we must not have too many bodies there. The more the bodies, more are our chances to be seen by the Green Man. In addition, I think we should reach there just 15 minutes before the deadline as the more the time we are there, more are our chances to be caught before we can manage to catch him.'

'But if we go there early, we will have a chance to warn the victim. What if the victim is already inside the warehouse when we are there, we will not be able to warn him.' Rajiv pitched in.

Everyone looked at Akash but he said 'I am not an expert in this. You guys should tell me if your force can stop the victim from getting killed, even if the victim does not know if it. My view is still the same, he will keep an eye on the victim and if we approach him, we expose ourselves.'

Rajiv said 'Our priority should be saving the victim and so we will go in early at 9.30 pm and that's final.'

Akash countered 'But what if Green Man is in disguise and we warn him that the Green Man is coming? We can't expect the Green Man to come in a green attire and we do not know the victim, so how do we distinguish between the Green man and the victim?'

The punchy cocktail of sarcasm and facts did the trick and left Rajiv having to agree to 'No Disclosure' plan.

Akash's word made sense and hence no one countered and Mr. Paik left the room along with Mr. Ghosh to arrange for logistics and support.

As the two police officers left the room, Rajiv quietly said to Akash 'Your ideas are very selfish and I see why. You are getting more hooked on to catching your Green Man but I am a police officer and people's safety will always be my top priority. I will first ensure that our victim is safe, then I can think of catching the criminal. Remember that.' Akash tried to explain 'No, You are getting me wrong Rajiv….' but Rajiv just gestured to Akash to talk to his hands and left the room.

Akash felt bad about Rajiv but he had much deeper things to worry about. He could not stop sweating at the thought of confronting the Green Man and resorted to coffee to dissolve his tensions. Rajiv on the other hand was cool as a cucumber. He was still angry with Akash but he had bigger priorities. He quickly took hold of his phone to catch up with his family, for no one knew if he would get a chance to speak to them again.

CHAPTER 21

Mr. Paik had only arranged for three more police officers and so the pack of seven made their way to China Town in a Scorpio. All of them were dressed in black, as they dress up in combat missions. The Warehouse was located around eight hundred meters off the main street. A lane moved inwards from the main street of China Town which mainly held Warehouses and factories on either side of it. This lane ended with the Rhino Warehouse main doors. This Warehouse was used as a chemicals factory at one time but it got closed as the owner was bankrupt. This factory land did not have valid papers. It was government property by papers but the owner claimed it was his property and put forward fake papers. A court case followed which is still running for the last five years. Hence, the factory has been left untouched since then.

Inside the main gate, there was a huge space for lorry parking. Akash thought to himself that at one time, this place must have held a minimum of fifteen Lorries at the same time. Few abandoned cars were also there, none was in usable condition. Both the side boundaries of the factory had huge bushes and trees covering around hundred feet from the boundary walls on both sides. This area was so dense that anyone could hide in the bushes without being seen. There were temporary huts in these bushes too, where the staff used to stay but they were not in livable condition anymore. Three hundred yards from the main door, the Warehouse structure laid perished. As per the map, the warehouse had five exits, one at the center and one by each sides. Mr. Paik revised the strategy to everyone. Two of the three police officers he brought with him would cover the back exits, the third police officer and Mr. Ghosh would cover the side exits in the front. Rajiv and Mr. Paik would go in through the middle entrance. As Akash had no experience of this kind of situation, he would stay back at the main gate and would guide the others over walkie-talkie.

By 9.45 pm, the team reached China Town but they could not have gone in through the main lane due to fear of detection. Mr. Paik had that covered too. They went through a parallel lane and entered an active factory. The factory was still running and there were workers inside. When they saw police officers approaching, they got scared and were about to disturb the silence when Mr. Ghosh gestured with his fingers, not to make any kind of abrupt noises. He called the manager forward and asked him to arrange for the door to be opened, which was nearest to the common wall of the factory with Rhino Warehouse. The manager had no clue what so ever and for once, his curiosities got the better of him as he asked what this was about? Mr. Ghosh responded sternly 'None of your business. You just make sure that there is no abrupt noise coming from your factory or else 'ak takeo charbo na', we will spare no one.'

The manager obediently opened the door, which led the gang to the common wall between the two factories. Using a ladder that they got from the factory, the team climbed the walls one by one and hopped on inside the Rhino's den. They had landed on the right side boundary wall of the factory.

Hundred feet of thick bushes, then they would land on concrete and then few meters and the warehouse structure would be at their footstep. A dim light could be seen inside the warehouse ground floor. The warehouse was two floor high but inside there were no flooring. There were machineries here and there and there were plenty of glass windows that were used for air ventilation. Most of the glass in the windows were broken, a toll taken by time and nature on the abandoned piece of land. There were rum and whisky bottles lying throughout the dense growth near the boundary wall, left overs of plenty of parties that take place in any unused and forgotten place in the lanes of Kolkata. The place was ideal for undisturbed drinking and looked like that the local lads have made good use of this. This kind of places are also supposed to attract passionate couples who prefer making love beneath the open sky rather than the fashionable and costly concrete boxes called hotels. Akash was very careful with his steps as either each step can land in something filthy or deadly as this kind of bushes can house many snakes too. Akash was himself amazed to see the amazing courage that he had developed lately throughout this case. A month back, even if someone paid him a full month's salary, he would not have gone in this kind of thick bushes at night in fear of snakes or who knows what other kinds, but now, not his health, but stealth and justice were his major concerns.

Mr. Paik posted one of his officers near the main gate so that he can remain in the bushes but still keep an eye out on the lane. The officer peeped through and reported that the lane had a few passer-by and at the other end of the lane, a group of punters were hanging out and there were few rickshaws parked in the lane, near the main gate of Rhino Warehouse.

It was five minutes passed 10 and all of them were patiently waiting in the bushes. Rajiv whispered 'Does anyone see anything inside the warehouse?'

Mr. Ghosh said, 'Yes I think I can see something moving, surely there is one or more than one person inside, should we go in and arrest them?'

Mr. Paik furiously responded 'What for? For chatting in an isolated place? We have to wait for the right time.'

Rajiv said 'And what is the right time, after he has killed the victim? I am again saying this, saving the victim's life is our top priority and we should attack now, when the victim is alive.'

Akash had lots to say but felt himself under ranked amongst so many police officers and hence kept quiet.

Mr. Paik again laid the law 'We can go and save the man but then we have to forget the chances of landing the Green Man. Even if we catch him in the act, his lawyer can find multiple ways to prove that he was just a trespasser and we will have no proofs against him.'

Akash could not resist opening his mouth as he whispered 'But we have the letters!'

Mr. Ghosh rubbished Akash's excitement by saying 'We don't even need a lawyer to junk the letters; even I can put enough justifications in court to scrap the letters. The letters does not say anything. We are here as we interpreted the letter in that way and that is not a proof. Anyone else can interpret it differently.'

Rajiv again said 'We have two minutes left to decide if we are saving or nabbing, you guys do whatever you want but I will save the victim. Whether you are with me or against me, it does not matter but anyone who will stop me is my enemy.'

Mr. Paik's voice rose louder than a whisper 'I am the police officer in charge here Mr. Rajiv. This is my city and so this is my case. All the police officers you see here are my police officers. I am responsible for their safety and I will not risk their lives just for nothing. I am also worried about saving the life of the victim and hence we are here, lets just plan it rather than going by our heart. Please be calm and help us plan this.'

Rajiv responded in a louder voice 'Plan! We should have planned before we come to the site and not at the site.'

Akash played the peacemaker, 'Everyone, please listen to me, we are two minutes away from the time in the letter, be it saving or nabbing, let's go to our positions, get a good view of what is happening and then lets act according to what we have in front of us. As we are not able to plan unified, let's just react unified.'

This worked as everyone calmed down and agreed and then Akash continued 'I never realized before coming here that this place would be so scary and so claustrophobic, I am literally pissing in my pants here and there is no place to hide if the action starts. I need a gun to stay safe, at least for self-defence or to scare someone away. Please Mr. Paik, please give a gun to me otherwise I may have a heart attack out of fear.'

Rajiv calmly said 'I told you before, he won't kill you, and he needs you as his challenger in this game. You have nothing to worry'

Akash said 'I hope that's true but I cannot be here out in the open with nothing but hope.'

Mr. Paik quickly analyzed the request and agreed that a gun would do many good to Akash's confidence and hence gave the gun to him and said 'Whatever happens, don't use it.'

Akash was left stunned but at that time, Mr. Paik's mobile phone started vibrating, the loud buzz sound seems to have carried afar as it broke the silence of the night. Mr. Paik quickly saw the whatsapp message and said 'They have found a common face in the video tapes. The man is in disguise but the face is common. Here, they have sent his photo over Whatsapp'. Rajiv and other joined in to look at the picture and exclaimed 'Isn't that the gardener at Mr. Ghora's home! We missed the bastard then but now, again, he is a few feet away. Let's nab him this time.'

The officer who was watching the lane suddenly reported to Mr. Paik that he is unable to see one of the rickshaw pullers in his rickshaw now. The man was sleeping in the rickshaw but now he is not here. If that is the Green Man, then he must have just now entered the warehouse complex. Mr. Paik quickly asked if the rickshaw puller looked like the man in the Whatsapp picture. The officer had his doubts but he responded positively that the rickshaw puller could be the man in Mr. Paik's phone.

CHAPTER 22

Elsewhere:

He expected a lot of visitors to the forgotten land of the Rhino Warehouse today, at a precise time. He wanted to keep a watch over the visitors without being seen and was surfing for the best options until he saw a rickshaw puller sleeping peacefully in his rickshaw. It struck him immediately. The most common and most non-threatening site at any Kolkata lanes is this. This is the perfect alibi to stay close to the action without raising any suspicion. He even thought of being a taxi driver sleeping in a taxi but a taxi at the end of a blind lane can raise suspicion and taxis come with numbers and can be traced back to the source, so he decided to be a rickshaw puller for the night. The action would not start before ten past ten at night but he needed to keep an eye out to check if all the invited parties are going to be there to his occasion. So, he went two hours early and parked his rickshaw by Rhino Warehouse. From 9 pm, he started to see some activities. A group of punters suspiciously gathered by the road end of the lane. They were laughing and rejoicing but they can well be police officers in disguise. In fact, no one in this lane can be excluded from suspicion. His fellow rickshaw pullers who joined by the time, can all be police officers.

He had another thing to look out for, where is the central character of the show for today. Where is the man, who is expected to be surrounded by demon and almighty all together, but the action that speak superior will sustain its place. He could see multiple passer-by coming close to the warehouse but eventually, they would go in some other factories. Around 9.45 pm, he finally had the glimpse of his target. A man in his 50s stepped down from a BMW and ordered his driver to leave. The man was indeed dressed up like a gentleman, with black suit over a blue shirt, giving him a smart look, though it goes unlike the scenario around. He was tall, only few inches short of six feet. His glasses made him look older than he actually was, may be because of the high-powered lenses he had in them. His nose was pointy and his face was speckled, giving him a decent look overall. As he gradually walked towards the warehouse entrance, his loud thumping boots, did leave an effect to its surroundings. The man finally approached the warehouse main gate, where he stopped for a moment, as if, analyzing his doom and gathering courage to step inside the game of death. He looked around for a while and even once had an eye contact with the man in the rickshaw, but he on the other side, acted as if he was actually sleeping. The man went in through a left-open hole on the wall, as the main door was jammed with uneven growth on it. Locals created this to have an easy access to this abandoned place for their private pleasures. He smiled to himself and said 'The bird's inside the net. Now let's find the heroes.'

Suddenly while making a move forward, he caught sight of a street beggar who was approaching towards the warehouse and did not have the trustworthy enough look. He got alarmed and stopped for a while again to watch the beggar's movements, till he saw the beggar walked past the warehouse area to the next street, pulled a blanket open and reclined just on the other side of the road. His heart was still pumping high as he still suspected the beggar may be a policeman in disguise and decided to keep an eye out for him. With the flow of time, and the meeting time approaching, there were no signs of the heroes he was waiting for. 'Surely, they could not crack the clue correctly, at least this much can I not expect of them!' he thought to himself and nodded his head in disappointment. It was eight minutes passed ten already and the challenger was nowhere on sight. He could not wait any longer as he had a more important and noble task to complete inside the warehouse and so; he let out a huge sigh of disappointment and stealthily, made his way towards the hole in the wall, and tried to avoid the sight of the beggar. Soon, he was inside the property and into the foot long grasses that had grown in the dark. He had entered through the left side of the property and from his position; he could faintly see the suited man waiting inside the warehouse. With a brisk pace, he made a move through the grasses but suddenly he became alarmed when he heard a buzz sound, seemed to be someone's mobile vibrating, scratching the silence and in fragment of seconds, he could spot a mobile screen glare illuminating the darkness from the bushes in the opposite direction. A witty smile beamed on his face and he spoke softly to himself 'So, the heroes are here'. He lent his ears towards the grasses and could hear low whispers of three or four distinct voices. He was very careful in his next steps and he slowly and slowly made his way towards the warehouse through darkness among the thick bushes.

CHAPTER 23

The police officers had just started to make their way to their posts as per Mr. Paik's plan. As they came near to the Warehouse, they could hear distinct voices of two people conversing from inside the warehouse. They were just hoping that the Green Man would not be able to see their movements. Akash stood back as he was already in his pre-defined post. He urged everyone to be careful. He was feeling this genuine rush of adrenaline inside him as the police officers got nearer to the Warehouse. They still could hear two distinct voices coming from the Warehouse and could even see two men standing face to face and they looked to be in a heated conversation. Rajiv whispered over walkie talkie as they gradually crawled towards the target 'We can still save the victim, that is our first priority.' Mr. Paik just nodded. Akash was new to this feeling. He had never been so anxious about anything and neither so scared. The gun in his hand only aggravated these feelings. He closely monitored the bunch of police officers and it was his responsibility to defend them from any danger. Suddenly, his spider sense tinkled. Something was wrong. He could sense something strange in the surrounding but was afraid enough to confirm his presumption to be true. He looked all around with his x-ray eyes and tried not to drop anything out of focus, until he saw a slight movement of a dark silhouette within the wild bushes opposite to his location. He took a step forward slightly and focused on the darkness where he thought he had seen something moving. This time, he could see it moving again but he was not sure of the object's appearance to be human figure or an animal. He pulled up his walkie talkie and said 'I think there is something on the opposite side of the bush. I think I can see slight movements.' Mr. Ghosh said 'That's the adrenaline getting to you. You are imagining boy, happens with the best of us on their first time.'

Akash did not say anything but continued to stare into the darkness. Again, he saw the bushes moving. This time, he put his fingers horizontally on his eyebrows so that the surrounding lights do not disturb his view and he stressed to see what laid beyond the darkness in the opposite bush. As he stressed his eyes into the darkness, a shiny metal thing and the hand holding it became barely visible. He was sure what it was as he was also holding the same thing in this hand, which Mr. Paik has just given to him. He boiled with excitement and fear but his words stopped in his mouth. He was so afraid that he was unable to voice his thoughts. He tried enough to alert his team over the walkie talkie but he just could not make through it. He tried hard to perorate through his visuals but felt numb from inside, in fear. He saw the shadow raising the gun and pointing it at someone, Akash was quick enough to drift his sight to find out the target. His brain went fatal and he could not believe it can be true and tried to re-focus again to be self-assured of what his eyes were trying to catch through, but that did not change anything. His hands turned cold in fear, all because the target was none other than the super-intendent of police, Rajiv. He was desperate to speak out now, he was trying to screech out his voice helplessly and save Rajiv but still, he could not. The harder he tried to break the shackles of his voice, the tighter his tongue got tied till he realized that the shadow is about to shoot Rajiv, who was unaware of the incumbent danger. Akash had no other options, no other plan ticked his head in that helpless moment, without thinking again for a second, he made a run out of the bush, raising his hand in the air. Just as he started his run, he got back his voice and all this inner pressure to speak out eventually got released and Akash shouted at the top of his voice 'GUN, GUN, Rajiiiiiv he has got a gun, save yourself, RUN RUN'.

All the officers were taken aback at Akash's sudden gesture, and Rajiv was pissed off by his kiddish behavior only till he saw Akash, running towards the opposite side of the bush with his gun up. Rajiv followed his run towards the darkness and spotted a glimpse of a dark figure through it. He and all the other police officers immediately pointed their gun towards the same object without even knowing its identity. But what they could only see was, a flash of movement of the dark object out of the Rhino warehouse through the hole in the entrance wall. There was too much chaos on the spot and Mr. Paik immediately ordered two of his officers to follow the shadow but there was only a range of commotion during this event, which must have disclosed to Green Man about their presence, and the Green Man would kill his victim any moment now.

As nothing worked as they planned, all of them were in utter confusion about their next steps as they did not have a plan B. There can be a roar of gun shot at any moment now, the thought of it chilled through their blood and Mr. Paik stood there like a zombie. Before anyone could speak out, Akash ordered 'We only have few second now to save the victim, Mr. Paik, Mr. Das (the only police officer among the three who were still on the spot) and Rajiv, you cover the front gates, Mr. Ghosh you go to the back by the right hand side and I will go to the back by the left hand side, quick' and Akash made a run towards the back gate. Everyone was stunned and any bit of leadership to follow a plan was better than no plans at all and so no one questioned and everyone just followed Akash's orders.

Akash was trembling as he went towards the back gate. He was totally being driven by his instincts. He did not have any clue what he will do if he faces the Green Man and neither did he have any clue about who was in the shadow. He only thanked himself that he had a gun and hoped he did not have to use it. He could hear a lot of chaos and commotion inside the warehouse and still not sure for whom he would be waiting by the exit door, the Green Man or the victim! At least he was assured that nobody is yet out of the building anyway. He was expecting to hear the sound of a lethal weapon or the cry of death anytime now. Within fraction of seconds, he managed to reach the backdoor on the left hand side and there was no one there yet, he called out to Mr. Ghosh and others but no one responded. He could not see anyone too as the angle of this gate made it hidden from all other gates. He slowed down his pace as he approached the gate, his gun pointed up, anticipating danger at any moment now. He had never perspirated so much in fear in his entire life, he felt like his body has warmed up to its highest temperature. His heart was pounding like it was going to have a heart attack and he could not find any way to control it's beats. Time seemed to be moving both fast and slow at the same time and he has been involved to the thick of it that he is in capable of planning anymore. All he was doing was out of the spur of moment, using pure basic survival instinct to drive the situation.

Akash felt like he can faint any moment now out of anxiety but unfortunately Almighty did not show any mercy on him, instead He challenged him with putting forward the queen of the chess board and said 'Check'. From the back door, which Akash was guarding, suddenly, he saw a masked figure running towards Akash. He had his face covered by a dark cloth and just when he saw Akash pointing his gun towards him, he brought out his own gun and flashed towards Akash, in the flash of a second. Akash was sure that he was facing his challenger, the Green Man and only hoped that Rajiv was right, the Green Man cannot kill his challenger, as he needed Akash. He just hoped that Rajiv was right for one fucking time. Akash again lost his speech. He tried to voice out his fear, shout out and alarm others about his moment of danger but all he could do was framing words within and gulp. He did not even know what to do after pointing the gun towards his opponent as if in a Russian stand off and so, just stood numb. His heartbeat throbbing hard enough like a wild animal trying to escape his chest.

He was 10 yards away from the Green Man and at that moment of time, Rajiv's screamed with joy (a contrast to Akash's state of mind) 'I got him, I got the victim. He is safe.' Both of them tried to locate Rajiv's voice, when Akash tried to sneak through the vision of danger, but before he could react, his ear's locked with a roar of gunfire, 'BAAANNGGGG'. Akash could feel the rush of pain flowing through his body. As he looked for the source, found his left hand elbow being hit by the bullet from Green Man's rifle and a thick flow of blood rushing down to the lower part of his body, forming a dark red pool beneath the ground, which he is managing to hold by his feet. The sight of which brought the thrush of voice back into Akash and he roared like a lion out of pain and fell down. The Green

Man looked once at Akash with an empathy, got assured that he will live to see another day, turned his back towards Akash, and started his retreat from the spot. At the sound of the revolver, everyone was coming to the spot from every direction. Akash felt that he is going to soon faint in pain or due to his massive rate of heartbeat but he cannot lose, he cannot lose after coming this close to the Green Man and even taking on a gunshot. He only needs to make the Green Man stay for five more seconds and then others will catch him. The Green Man had already started to pick up pace and was soon going to be over the back boundary wall of the Rhino Warehouse and be gone in the shadows forever. Again by instinct, in the deep pain he was in, Akash raised his rifle, pointed towards the Green Man, and pressed the trigger, 'BAAAANNNGGG' and then, as if from the recoil of his shot, he fainted.

CHAPTER 24

Elsewhere:

He was sitting in a room with just a table in his front and two empty chairs opposite to him. There was a light above his head and only one door in the room. His hands were handcuffed to the chair and he saw the door opening. Three police officers came in, one of them bringing an extra chair with him. He knew all of them by face but not by name. The one who looked to be in charge introduced himself as ACP Rajiv Mehta and he introduced the others as Mr. Dhole and Mr. Paik. Now he could relate those faces he knew to a name. He felt his nerves at the police station interrogation room, being there for the first time ever, but had to put on courage to say 'Why am I brought here Mr. Mehta? I need my lawyer.'

Rajiv calmly said 'All you need now is to listen to us and answer our questions. You were arrested from the crime scene at Rhino Warehouse and you endangered a police mission. So shut the fuck up and answer our damn questions. Why were you in two different crime scenes of Mr. Khan and Mr. Ghora's death, in two different cities and why were you in Mr. Ghora's home as a gardener?'

He just replied 'Because it's my job. As a media person, it's my job to be at crime sites.'

Rajiv got up from his chair and was about to slap him tight out of his suppressed rage but Mr. Paik stopped Rajiv and said 'He is not going anywhere, he will be here only till he answers all our questions, so lets take it slow and start from the basics. We will cover everything but let's go one by one. He will answer everything truthfully Rajiv, won't you lad?'

Mr Paik turned his attention to him but he was scared as hell with Rajiv's advance to hit him. He just nodded his head.

Rajiv took back his seat and restarted 'Ok, let's start from basic then, What's your name?'

'Mr. Shankar Roy'

'So Mr. Roy, what do you do for living?'

'I was a media journalist.'

'Was?'

'Yes, I lost my job recently due to a court case.'

'Do you care to explain to put more details on this court case?'

'My wife, Damini Roy, filed a court case against me that I torture her and that case caught the attention of the media as I was a reputed media reporter. She had gathered video evidence of me, slapping her, using his sex toy, detective Akash Bose whereas she had….'

Rajiv snapped 'Hang on, hang on, Detective Akash Bose as in, from Bangalore!'

Shankar got scared again and replied, 'Yes, the private detective with whom all of you were driving this case till now.'

Rajiv got out of his seat 'Oh my God! Oh my God! You are related to Akash, Oh fucking God!'

Mr. Dhole said 'Ooohhh now I remember, the impotency case for which Akash was accused by court for gathering false documents. You are the defendant in that case! Mr. Shankar Roy, ok now everything is coming to a full circle in my head.'

Rajiv just looked stunned at Mr. Dhole whereas Mr. Paik was just expressionless. Mr. Paik raged to Mr. Dhole and Rajiv 'And when were you planning to tell this crucial detail about Akash to me? Such a crucial detail should have been in Line Number 1 when you are introducing Akash. Hi, this is Akash, he has a criminal background of forging documents in court.'

Mr. Dhole put a shameful face and said 'Sir, I, I, I thought you have seen it in the newspaper or news, Sir.'

Mr. Paik was shouting like he was molested 'Do you have to be a RAW agent to figure out that Bangalore news does not feature in Kolkata!'

Mr. Dhole had already sunk his head as much as his fat neck could allow, he tried to sulk more but his neck refused. He just said 'Sorry Sir, I thought…… Sorry Sir, Akash is a nice guy, it was just a mistake from…'

Mr. Paik was again going to shout but Rajiv calmed down the situation Mr. Paik, I know how it looks like but the case was not that bad. He did it to protect a lady from harm as he was trapped by the lady to believe that Mr. Shankar used to regularly torture her physically.'

Then Rajiv turned to Mr. Shankar and said 'Mr. Shankar, can you please explain the full story again, with all minute details and how Akash was involved in it. So that myself and Mr. Paik can be fully aware of the case as I am also half aware of the full details.'

'I married Damini three years ago but could never give her proper time and attention despite of her numerous silent urge and plead towards it, due to the busy and unpredictable schedules in my profession. I often traveled to other cities with less than a day's notice or sometimes even immediately after receiving a heads-up over a call at the middle of the night. With my work being the first priority, I could barely get an opportunity to spend any precious moment with my wife. I promised to her multiple times that I would spend an evening with her or take her out for a movie the next day or go for shopping, followed by dinner. However, multiple times during these dates, I could not keep up the promise as planned, due to sudden work commitments or emergencies that came through during the course of the day. I was proficient at my job and had sufficient fame and influence too but the more you put your heart into your work life, the lesser is the space remaining in your personal life. A police officer as yourself would surely understand my problems better as both our professions bump with this common work challenges and gifts similar personal life challenge, which means, a very disturbed family life. I asked her to apply for jobs or take up some hobby but she always denied, saying that, if she becomes busy in her life, then it will lessen the chance to even meet with each other, which she won't be able to afford. I failed to interpret her indication towards the serious mental depression she was going through due to lack of attention. This carried on until she could not take it anymore. Neither she nor my in-laws ever informed me that Damini had a serious relationship pre-marriage and her boyfriend even approached my in-laws for marriage. My in-laws were very conservative about religion issues, they did not encourage the proposal further, moreover manipulated Damini and forced her to tie a knot with me. Soon, Damini moaned on this decision even more, as I could not give her proper attention, which she deserved. I failed to realize that her inner pain and urge to be loved, would not be bounded by any nuptial bonds anymore. I did try to give her as much time as my job offered to, but I had no words to justify myself when I could not. Damini had always suppressed her emotions and never complained too much about it but I do regret it now and I wish she had cried out her pain, loud enough, for me to have a reality check and would have also given me an opportunity further, to mend it before tearing it apart. I regret every day, to have missed all the clear signs, which I knowingly ignored.'

Shankar paused for a while, hoping for questions but no one asked any. All were silently waiting for Shankar to resume and so he did.

'My nightmares soon became reality. My wife started having an affair with her Ex. She was betraying me and I had no clue about it. She must have loved her newly revived love life as she looked much fresh and happy all the time. She has revived her lost youth, she was not sulking around me anymore and was out of the house, most of the time. She started to take care of herself, took up a hobby and started looking presentably beautiful with the desired smile I always wished to look up to, but sadly I did not know that I was not the reason behind any of it. She never had to lie much to me as most of the time she was alone, but whenever asked, she always had an excuse ready, which was strong enough to be not questioned further. I became relaxed and happy. Finally, for unknown reasons, my marriage life had taken a turn for good. I did not know it had taken a completely wrong turn. This continued for a few months until she decided to permanently reside on the happy island she had just been a part off.'

Mr. Dhole looked confused 'What Island! Where did this Island come from?'

Rajiv again gave a tough look to him and said 'The Island is her Ex, it's a metaphor, and don't you get to hear such metaphors in news Mr. Dhole?'

Mr. Dhole again resorted to sulking and Shankar continued.

'She was desperate to be with her Ex but she needed a divorce for that. Like everyone in this society, no one wants to be the bad person but they want the bad outcome. She wanted a divorce but not on the grounds of having an affair. Therefore, she set up a drama. She plotted a divorce on grounds of physical abuse and hence, she reached out to Akash Bose, your famous private detective and FUCKED him. My wife slept with your asshole sidekick, Akash, so that she could manipulate him to help gather evidence in our divorce case. After sleeping with him, she set me up to physically abuse her.'

Rajiv interrupted 'Are you sure that your wife….. you know, like, with Akash, did they…'

Shankar said 'I am 100% sure he fucked her, why else would he put his reputation and career on the line to forge documents in a media hyped court case. He very well knew the risk he was taking and why would he take that risk, if he were not physically involved with her? Would anyone take that much of risk just for a normal client?'

Rajiv found logic in Shankar's justification and asked him to continue.

'That night, Akash had setup camera outside my window to film me abusing her. I had never ever come close to physically abuse my wife, so it would take her a lot of persuasion to make me hit her. She had arranged for all the evidences so that she can get caught on cheating me. She knew that I was coming from an office party that night and so, I would be drunk. So, she chose that night. When I came, the first thing my eyes fell on was a colorful-chequered men's under pants lying on my sofa. I did not have any colorful ones and so, immediately, I fell into her trap. I questioned her about it and she acted as if, she had been caught on the act and confessed that she was having an affair with her Ex lover and they had made love on that couch and on my bed that night, few minutes before I had come home. I was enraged and shouting at her but still I fell short of her expectation that I could hit her. As I reacted to the news, she got enraged too and made me feel the warmth of the sofa as she told me minute details of how they made love, naked, on my sofa, thirty minutes before I came in. I still did not hit her, I wanted to, I badly wanted to but I could not still hit her and I just asked her 'Why?' She responded 'Because he can make me scream out in pleasure, because he can make me suck him. I have never sucked you but he wets me so much, that I cannot stop sucking him. You never ever satisfied me on bed but when he pushes inside me, I feel this pure bliss, I just can't open my eyes and I can't stop biting him and scratching the bed till he fills my insides.' Then she laid down on the sofa to show me all the postures in which they betrayed me. She carefully did this so that it is not filmed as Akash was filming the back end of the sofa. I could not control myself but I still did not hit her but I could not stop myself when she opened her boobs to show me love marks. The love bites were all around her neck and everywhere. Finally, she won, I hit her as I could not take it anymore.'

Mr. Paik said 'Do you have the video with you which Akash took?'

Shankar answered 'I always carry my doom with me, it's in my mobile.'

Mr. Paik ordered Mr. Dhole to uncuff Shankar's hands and as they were uncuffed, Shankar opened his mobile and showed them the video. The video justified all that Shankar had described. But as it had no audio. Unless one knew the story, which Shankar has just now shared, it can only be related as a heated argument where the wife is more animated, like all family arguments. This one ended with Shankar slapping Damini as he could not tolerate Damini's animations anymore.

'What happened then?' enquired Mr. Paik.

'As the divorce case followed and the video evidence was shown, it was all over the internet and news. I was trolled everywhere and I even lost my job. As it dealt with a reporter, the rivals of my channel rolled it as Breaking News. I was in every news, slapping my wife. My life was ruined, everyone around me though that I used to physically abuse my wife. Damini gained the sympathy she wished for. The police continuously harassed me and so did the media and my in laws and neighbors, no one spared me for any sympathy. The court case went on but no one cared about it. Everyone had made his or her presumption about me. My lawyer was able to prove the truth and the situation for which I had to raise my hand but everyone thought it to be a lawyer's way of manipulating the truth. So, no one cared about what the judge had to say but Damini understood that she would lose the divorce case. Damini asked her lawyer to put impotency reasons for divorce. The court asked for my impotency test and Akash bribed the doctor and forged the test reports to prove that I am impotent. Damini showed the report and got the divorce. The news flashed everywhere, that Mr. Shankar Roy is an impotent. I was totally broken, I even though of committing suicide but I could not do it. I was desperate to tell my story to the world. So, when the divorce settled and Damini had robbed me of fifty lacs of alumni, I trapped her, the same way she trapped me. Tit for Tat. After all, I am a journalist and an expert in sting operations. In the name of one last party, I got Damini drunk and pulled up the topic of why she divorced me. She already had the divorce and the court case was over and hence had turned down her guard and confessed to everything, even to Akash forging the impotency documents. I arranged to make the confession viral and finally, tasted revenge. Although my life was ruined but at least I had the last laugh and I had cleared my public image. Damini left the country and so the media took the revenge on Akash and screwed his life.'

CHAPTER 25

Rajiv just looked blankly at Mr. Dhole and said 'You missed to give me all these details about Akash!'

Mr. Dhole's act of sulking continued with no near end. Rajiv questioned to Shankar 'Do you think Akash knew about this extra marital relationship of your wife? Or did he love her too?'

Shankar literally spited 'How many more men are going to love my wife! I don't give a damn about whether he loved her or not. I just hate him. He screwed my life and every time I look at him, I can picture him naked, fucking my naked wife while she moans in pleasure. You don't know what it feels like. I feel like killing him every second of my life.'

Rajiv said 'That's a dangerous confession to make during a police interview. It can be used against you. Anyways why didn't your wife get married to her Ex after the divorce?'

'Oh, I did not tell you about that Karma? When Damini approached her Ex to marry her, he confessed that he was already married and loves his wife. He was just using Damini for pleasure. How cool is that. That is one of the only good things that happened in this case. Damini may have got the money but she never got the love she was chasing for. She betrayed me to find happiness in her life but her life got screwed too. Both of us got shattered and that too, together.'

'What is the name of her Ex and where does he live?'

'I don't know, I don't want to associate a face with that person in my mind. Then I will have the same nightmares about him and Damini making out, as I had for Akash and Damini. Damini only told that his name is Samir. She did not give an address as I did not ask for one.'

Mr. Paik broke his silence 'But it still does not explain why you were at the murder sites and at Mr. Ghora's home as a gardener.'

Shankar said 'It's a long story. I did not have any job or any way to get back to journalism. No one would consider me, even with my qualification, on further background check and also I had lost all my wealth and savings to pay for the court case and the alumni. I had lost everything and did not have a penny left. I was doing delivery jobs to pay for my expenses and boiling for revenge. The only satisfaction I felt was whenever I saw Akash on the news, being harassed by the media and public for providing false evidence in court against me. Then, one day, I received a phone call from an unknown number. A husky voice said 'Be at Hotel S.M.S site tomorrow morning. It's going to be a big news.' I said that I am not a reporter anymore and asked why is he telling this to me. The voice responded 'Giving you, first media rights so that you can taste sweet revenge against Akash Bose.' and cut the line. I could not figure out who it is, I tried to trace the number and find out about the sim owner but failed due to limited resources and contacts. Wasn't even sure if it was just a prank! Anyways, even if I caught some news, no one would publish it, so I called few of my fellow reporters and tipped them. I managed to earn some commission against this as I was badly in need for money. Also, if it was a prank call, I would not be pranked. So, it was a win-win for me.'

Everyone else in the room looked surprised. Rajiv was the first one to speak out 'Did you ever find out who was this stranger? Why did he have against Akash? Did he contact you again? Why did he call you only? Mr. Paik, check the number he is referring and trace it. I want full information about it. So, this Green Man knew Akash well before the murder of Mr. Khan.'

Mr. Paik nodded but Shankar only responded 'I have already answered your questions inspector.'

Mr. Dhole started now 'So, someone tipped you to go there, to ruin Akash's image more? But what was there to ruin? It only made Akash a hero in the media. All it ruined was the image of my police force.'

Shankar shrugged his soldier and stayed silent till Mr. Dhole coaxed again for an answer. Shankar finally said 'May be the Green Man thought that Akash would not be able to solve the case that he has taken and the body would be found by police. A person murdered in his first missing case, would ruin his career even more.'

Mr. Dhole looked quite angry now and said 'Ok, but why did you not try to find who called in for such a suspicious news, or why didn't you later realize that how did the caller know about the murder even before it took place or why didn't you inform anything to the police?'

Shankar responded 'I did, I tried to find out all I could about the number and wondered through several hours, about possible list of callers that could inform me regarding this! But I could not come across any valid result to my thoughts and hence concluded that there was nothing to report to the police as it was just a tip and I made decent money from it, so I just went along with it.'

Suddenly Mr. Paik thrashed his fist to the table and exploded 'Then why were you in the murder site? Why did you go to Hotel S.M.S in disguise?'

'I just could not feed my curiosity. I had to know what it was about. I had to take the pleasure of witnessing Akash fail at something and getting media shamed. Also, I could direct the reporters towards Akash's failure from the spot and so I had to go there. Everyone in the city and the media knew me and I did not want attention to divert from Akash and so I went in disguise, so that I can kill my curiosity and do my bit to ruin Akash's life further more. I went there, tipped the media to keep their cameras on Akash and it worked. The blabbermouth rookie could not cover up the serial killer story and the media over heard it, how can this kind of an amateur be a private detective!'

Rajiv asked Mr. Dhole 'How did Akash find the body among all the police officers you had on the field?'

Mr. Dhole said 'Most of the police officers were busy blocking the media and we only had four police officers searching the field. I divided the area into five divisions and allocated one area to search for each of the officers and Akash. Luckily, the body was in Akash's area.'

Mr. Paik said 'Ok, so did this stranger call you again to inform about Mr. Ghora?'

Shankar responded shyly 'No, I got that information from all of you officers.'

As usual, Rajiv was the first one to react 'What! We have a mole among us! Tell me immediately who that is or I will smash your face right now Mr. Shankar.'

Shankar got scared again and quickly added 'No, No, Sir, not like that. When the news of the serial killer was doing the rounds and Akash was named as the challenger to the serial killer, I thought that I can get a lot of information from Akash but obviously, I could not face him directly. You do not know us reporters Sir, we go crazy for the story that we are following. We can go to any extent to follow that story. My reporting days might have been over but the reporter inside me would not let me stop. The commission that I earned from the last tip lured me towards it but more importantly, I could not resist this story as it can show to everyone that how much incapable Akash really is. I was sure that he is a joke of a detective, a very stupid guy and I was desperate to prove it. So, I kept on following him for days to understand his schedule and one day, when he was not supposed to be in his house, I went in, disguised as an old man trying to meet Akash to discuss about a marriage proposal with my imaginary daughter. His maid opened the door for me. I waited for the right opportunity and as soon as I got it, I bugged the place with a microphone inside an used alcohol bottle.'

Mr. Dhole exclaimed 'Maa ki aankh! So, you could hear everything that we were saying when the first letter arrived. Oh my God! I am placing you under arrest for that one.'

Mr. Paik added 'Did you know that a letter was going to arrive? Did anyone inform you about it? Be truthful as we will check your phone records and phone location to cross verify everything you are saying.'

Shankar said 'No, I was not. I had no clue what so ever but I sensed that if any action was to happen to this case, it is going to happen via Akash and so, I kept an eye and ear on him. I know it is not the right thing to do but we do this all the time in our line to get news.'

Mr. Dhole was still furious 'We have a righteous criminal here. He knows it is not right but still did it because he had to. Now rotten in jail you asshole.'

Shankar looked up to Mr. Dhole with doleful eyes but even that was not enough to melt Mr. Dhole's anger.

Mr. Paik asked 'What happened next?'

Shankar said 'I heard the name of the second victim from over hearing your discussions about the letter. When your team left for Kolkata, I immediately decided to follow you but I could not head up to the police station, so I thought that I had my best chances to be close to the crime. If I could monitor Mr. Ghora's house and check on his schedules, that would surely help me. . So, I started observing their house from outside and saw that they have a huge garden, without anyone taking care of it. I dressed up as a gardener and began ploughing their garden alongside monitoring the house. The role of a poor gardener gave me a simple excuse even if the Ghora family would catch me. I would simply justify myself being poor and show my desperation in the job and ask them for money. But before I could make much progress, your team arrived in Mr. Ghora's house and I had to flee as Akash can recognize me anytime.'

Mr. Paik regretted 'And while fleeing, you also bugged my shoes with a microphone! So, if only I had shown the Whatsapp message of your picture to Akash yesterday night at the Rhino Warehouse, we could have resolved it then and there.'

Mr. Paik shrugged his shoulders in apology for disturbing the flow of confession and Shankar started again. 'I had no direction or clue to go to anymore and hence, I just kept an eye on Akash and Rajiv Sir. I stayed at the same hotel as them, in the opposite room of Akash and continuously monitored their movements. I saw them go to bed that night and thought the action was over for the night. Then in the dead of night, I heard some commotion and followed your movements. As you left the hotel, I followed you officers to Mr. Ghora's murder site. I dressed myself up as a villager, moved around in the murder site, and gathered some critical news and footages. The Green Man news was hot property in the media market and so, I made quite a good money from it.' Shankar finally had something to smile about and so, he beamed.

Mr. Paik said 'How did you know about Rhino Warehouse, did you over hear that too?'

Shankar said 'No, not that one. Well I wanted to but there were too much police around for me to eaves drop on your hotel door. I was about to book my return tickets but I received a call from the Green Man again and he asked me to be in Rhino Warehouse at 10 minutes passed 10 at night. He said it would be the biggest news of my life.'

Rajiv shouted 'This is so messed up, sometimes he calls and sometimes he does not, what's going on here! Why would the Green Man want him to be at the Rhino Warehouse?'

Mr. Paik said 'So that he can be a witness that the police lost and he won, when he kills his victim.'

Rajiv counter questioned 'Then why not in Mr. Ghora's case?'

Mr. Paik thought and then said 'May be he was monitoring Shankar and he knew that Shankar already knew about it!'

Rajiv turned his attention to Shankar 'Why did you want to shoot me in the darkness? Why did you point the gun at me?'

'Shoot you! Gun! What are you saying? I do not have any gun?'

Rajiv answered 'Akash shouted that you are pointing a gun at me from the darkness. That's why I pointed my gun at you. When you ran away, my officers chased you down and brought you here.'

Shankar shaked his body in frustration 'When is that detective going to stop ruining my life? I did not have any gun! I came in to the Warehouse a lot early and dressed as a rickshaw puller. I monitored the warehouse but no one got in except one suited guy who I thought to be the business man who was going to get killed.'

Rajiv furiously interrupted 'And you did not step out to inform him about his life threat! You pig!'

Shankar defended himself 'I was dealing with a serial killer who kills for no personal reasons. I was scared Sir, I was scared as anything. I thought if I swayed from his instructions, surely I would be the next target. I went inside the warehouse in the mentioned time and suddenly I saw movements and mobile flashes from the opposite side of the bush. I was sure it was your team there. I wanted to capture the whole rescue operation in my camera and so, I brought out my camera slowly and started shooting your team. You can check my camera records too, I had shot for 5 or 6 seconds when suddenly Akash came out of the bushes, shouting. I got scared as all of your attention turned towards me. I made a run for it outwards of the warehouse but soon your police officers caught up with me, hit me in the back, and arrested me. After that, I remember nothing till I find myself here.'

Rajiv composed down 'So, Akash thought your camera to be a gun as both were shiny metal and would shine a bit in the darkness. Obviously, he did not expect media there and so, he rightly thought that you are pointing a gun at me and shouted to save me. I just can't keep on hating that lad, he somehow impresses me all the time.'

Shankar said with very high hopes 'I heard he got shot, is he dead?'

Mr. Paik responded 'No, he is recovering in the hospital; the bullet hit his left arm, so he will live, in fact, he will live quite well. Unlike you.'

Shankar counter questioned 'And what about the second shot that I heard?'

Rajiv proudly said 'Our boy stopped the Green Man from escaping with that one. That shot hit Green Man's left belly and dropped him. We called an ambulance, took him to the hospital but the man 'died again' before reaching there.'

Shankar said 'What do you mean that he 'died again'?'

Rajiv laughed and said 'As a sweet revenge for messing our plot at the Rhinos, let's keep you guessing on that one and you can live on with the suspense.'

Rajiv and Mr. Paik and Mr. Dhole got off their seat and Mr. Paik asked Mr. Dhole to validate all that Shankar had said. Rajiv asked 'Do you think he is telling the truth?'

Mr. Paik said 'I have interrogated many liars but this one definitely is not lying. He sounded most genuine. I believe him and his phone records and locations should validate his story. I think it will come out all fine.'

Mr. Dhole paused for a moment and said 'What do you think about what Shankar has done? Is it justified? I mean if we were in his shoes, would we be doing the same thing?'

Rajiv said '100%, anyone messes with my family, I would kill him. I would say, he went quite lenient on Akash, as he never harmed him physically. What Akash did cannot be pardoned. He broke a family.'

Mr. Dhole said 'Let's not conclude things before we flip the coin and hear Akash's version too.'

Rajiv reacted angrily 'What version! Do you want to hear how he made Damini moan! There is nothing to hear anything from him. Its making me sick, just to think about what he has done.'

Mr. Paik played the peacemaker again 'Yeah we will do that and we will also confront him once he gets back to sense but for now, our business is not over and I am getting too anxious to see what else this case holds. Let's go and talk to our second catch of the night.'

CHAPTER 26

The three police officers shifted rooms from the interrogation room to Mr. Paik's office where the man (in suit) they had rescued from Rhino Warehouse was waiting for them. As Mr. Paik saw him reclined in his office, he quickly begged an apology for the long wait and said 'We just wanted to have some words with you about yesterday night Mr. Debasis Sen. Would you please brief us why you were there at Rhino Warehouse?'

Rajiv had a quick look at Mr. Debasis Sen whom they had safeguarded from the Green Man's claw last night at Rhino Warehouse. His face and hands had some minor scratches and cuts, may be, due to the mild conflict on the scene. His decent appearance doesn't replicate him to be an honest man, his eyes shows he is trying to hide his original self and must have a darker side of him as well. By his behavior and reactions in front of the cops, Rajiv apprised that Mr. Debasis Sen knows well how to conceal his dark image, and get his jobs done in silence. He also assumed that Mr. Sen still have many faithful dogs to protect him from danger as his eyes look confident enough.

Debasis said in a very confident voice 'No problem officer. Well, if it was anything else, I would have thought before I speak, but I understand the seriousness of this context and so I am going to come clean. I hope this conversation is not being recorded and these words will not be used against me?'

Mr. Paik pushed the pause button in the recorder in front of them and said 'Now, they won't. Please feel free to talk to us. We will let you know once we resume recording.'

Debasis resumed 'I have a construction project planned which is not getting municipal corporation approval as we need to cut down huge number of trees to free up space for our 80 acre construction site. I didn't have a valid ownership document, it was a forged one. Henceforth, I have been trying for a long time to get a green signal from The Corporation and I have already fed them a lump sum in advance. But, still the procedure kept delaying and they even started asking for more inducements to speed up the procedure. Then one day, I suddenly got a call from an unknown number and that person introduced himself as Mr. Madan Biswas, a middleman who can arrange a meeting with the Head of the District Municipal Corporation, Mr. Chatterjee, who would be able to facilitate the approval of my project. He also advised me to bring whole sum sweetener to make the District Head happy enough to agree on the same day, and to show my desperation on receiving approval. He suggested me to not bring any companion, to avoid disclosure of the matter in public, which will bring more harassment rather than agreement to the procedure.'

Rajiv interrupted 'And you fell for it! Knowing that there is a killer out there killing business men who had harmed the environment, still you agreed to go and that too alone?'

Debasis said 'I had never committed anything to pollute the environment before this. I thought the killer would go for someone who has already hurt the nature, not someone who is planning to. I did not expect the killer to know of my plans and frankly, I never thought, before now, that I am actually harming the environment and in the long run, my own future generation.'

Rajiv shook his head in frustration and said 'Continue, please.'

Debasis obeyed 'Mr. Madan Biswas said that he had somehow urged Mr. Chatterjee to meet me once so that I get a chance to present my proposal to him. If he finds it credible, Mr. Chatterjee will arrange for the approvals. Madan also said that he himself would take 50 lacs as his fees. I have been to multiple secret meetings like this in my past and everyone happened like this only. There looked to be nothing wrong and so I agreed to meet them at the abandoned Rhino Warehouse site, as it was secretive. I came along a lot early as my previous meeting ended earlier than expected. When I went in, I did not find any open doors at the front. I looked for some time and tried to unlock the front doors but they did not budge. So, I found an open window in the front and jumped about 7 feet down to get inside the Warehouse and then I waited for Mr. Madan there.'

Mr. Paik asked 'When did he show up? And can I turn on the recording now?'

Debasis nodded in agreement and answered 'Just about 10 pm. He wore a mask and so I could not recognize who he was but as soon as I saw the mask, I knew I was in deep trouble. I knew about the serial killer killing Ashish as he harmed Mother Nature. I realized then that I too was guilty of that offence but never ever imagined that I would be a target for that. As soon as I saw a masked man, my fears knew no bound and I was about to shout and scream and run. I had never ever been so afraid in my entire life.

Mr. Dhole hadn't spoken for a long time now and had to speak 'But the police force did not hear any scream! Surely, he could not have come close to you and stop you from screaming. If the police force had heard your scream, then they would have rushed in and saved you and caught the killer alive.'

Mr. Paik and Rajiv gave an angry glare at Mr. Dhole and then urged Debasis to continue.

Debasis obeyed again 'As soon as the masked man realized that I was about to scream, he put his hands up in the air to show me that his hands are not holding anything sharp or a gun, he urged me to be patient and said to me 'Deba, Deba, please, please calm down, calm down, please do not scream.'

Mr. Paik looked surprised and said 'And you did not scream? Just because he said 'please'!'

Rajiv said 'He knew you!'

Mr. Dhole said 'You should have screamed and we could have caught him alive.'

Debasis sounded annoyed but he continued 'No I did not scream, because I knew that voice, I knew who that masked man was when he called me Deba. Very few people call me by that name. But he could not be the same person, it was impossible.'

Mr. Paik urged 'Why? Why was it impossible?'

Debasis said 'Because it was the voice of Ashish Ghora, who died at the car accident, who was killed by the serial killer.'

No one gave away any signs of surprise. Rajiv and his team had their share of shock long before, when they found out in the Rhino Warehouse that the killer inside the Warehouse was Mr. Ashish Ghora as they had taken his body to the hospital (where he was pronounced dead) after he was shot down by Akash. So, everyone else in the room apart from Debasis looked quite composed and they just said 'How did you know Ashish?'

'Back in our early days, myself and Ashish, both used to sell marijuana and all other illegal stuffs. Ashish was my biggest rival but he had a sharp business mind. He always managed to snatch the big orders from me and always was better than me in running the marijuana and other illegal business. I tried a lot to beat him in business but he always got the better of me. He expanded his business to multiple cities whereas I only operated in Kolkata. I desperately wanted to beat him but always fell short. I even tried to kill him off but he got to know of it and thrashed my gang and me as if we were mosquitos. I could not beat him with muscle, so, I played my gamble. I asked the locals to lure him to be an MLA. Ashish caught the bait. He thought he was going to be more powerful as an MLA but I had different plans.'

Mr. Dhole knew no stopping 'So, you made him an MLA! How can that help you? You only gave him more power!'

Rajiv said rudely 'Mr. Dhole, would you mind not interrupting him?'

Mr. Dhole felt very humiliated and shut up.

Debasis took the opportunity of the silence to continue. He needed no coaxing 'As soon as he became an MLA, he was a public figure. I used to tip media about his criminal operations and the media crushed him. They repeatedly ran news about the new MLAs illegal businesses. Even the public turned against him and so, the party had to turn against him too. Due to the recurring news, the people and the pressure from the party, he could not control his illegal businesses anymore and left it to his right hand, Bikram Pal to handle his business. I kept the media pressure on and I bought Bikram. Within days, I manipulated all his goons to join my side and I took over his business. In this line, whoever has the muscle runs the show. Ashish was already in deep waters with the reporters, the public and his party. He did not see this betrayal coming. When he did, he did not have the muscle power anymore to do anything about it. Soon, I took over all of his illegal businesses and his party thrashed him out as he was drawing too much negative publicity. Within months, I took away everything from him.'

Finally Debasis paused, with pride.

Rajiv analyzed the situation and said 'So, you ruined his life and he had good reasons to kill you. He must have waited all this time to plot to kill you. But if Ashish Ghora did not die on the car crash, who did? CCTV footage confirmed that Ashish was driving the car and there was no one with him.'

Debasis said 'Exactly! When I realized it was him, I had the biggest shock. I asked to confirm if it was really him, as I knew that the serial killer killed him. He just laughed and continued to laugh.'

'Then he said and I quote it 'Don't you get it still, I am the serial killer you asshole, I killed myself so that I do not get life sentence and spend the rest of my life inside prison.' I was stunned as anything. I just looked at him and he continued to read my expressions and laugh. If he was the serial killer and I was tricked to be here, then surely he is planning to kill me. I kept sweating and nearly pissed on my pants.'

Debasis paused to catch breath and some water from a jar in the table but Mr. Paik was too anxious to deal with silence now and he urged 'If he is still alive then whom did he kill in the car accident and how?'

Debasis could only finish half of the glass and he had to resume 'I too asked him the same question about how he managed to fake his death, to which he responded and I quote 'that was the best part of the game. From the day Bikram betrayed me, I was waiting to take my revenge. I became friends with him so that I can gain his trust and one day, use it to wipe him off the face of the earth. Anyone betraying Ashish Ghora is already destined to die in my hands. Just like you. Bikram made it quite easy for me to finish him. As soon as I came to know that, the police had decoded the letter that I placed in the house of detective Akash Bose and had come to my house to save me from the serial killer, I immediately invited Bikram to go to Digha with me for a party. He happily agreed. While returning, I slipped a strong slipping pill in his drinks and soon, he fainted. I put him in the floor of the back seat of my car and put a cloth around him so that he would not be visible to the toll officer. I could not afford to put him in the dicky of the car as he was very heavy and I am quite old to carry someone around in my arms. In the toll station, I initiated a small conversation with the toll officer so that he can be my evidence that I was traveling alone. Once I was in clear road, I parked my car and then took my revenge. I smashed his face with a rock till it was beyond recognition.' At that point, officers, you should have looked at his expression. His eyes turned red with the thought of revenge and his lips parted ways to give a grin.'

'Then he again continued 'Once I had killed him, I put Bikram in the driver seat. Then I put petrol over my car and lit the car on fire. The fire itself did the rest of the work. I took no chance; I killed him before the fire as I could not take any chance of his face being recognized. Otherwise, I would have loved to see him burn alive. I had planted my documents in Bikram's jeans and Bikram's face was too much damaged and burnt to be recognized. Bikram is a low class criminal who would not be missed from society and by God's grace; he was of the same age and build as me. It worked fine in every ways. Even if people found out that it's Bikram, I could re-appear and make an alibi that I was never in the car. I had nothing to lose anyways; the judge was surely going to sentence me to lifetime prison. I had my revenge and got back my life. Only thing sad is that I would not be able to be with my family again but one must sacrifice something to get something. I would not have been able to stay with my family if I landed up in jail too.''

Rajiv was shocked 'Oh my fucking God! That son of a bitch tricked his death and fooled us. What happened then?'

Debasis said 'He just could not stop laughing looking at me shaking in fear. I was shocked as anything. Bikram was a close friend of mine, his death was a shock, finding a dead man in front of me was a greater shock and on top of it, and then there was the fear of him killing me. He would surely kill me anytime now. If he can kill Bikram who was also his friend, I was only his enemy. Always.'

Debasis continued 'Suddenly he stopped laughing as if something has just now struck him, may be a new idea on how to kill me. I was staring at death and lost for words. Then he looked at me and surprisingly asked 'Tui ekhane kikore eli?''

Mr. Paik translated that to others 'It means, how you came here?'

Debasis continued 'I showed him the broken window in the Warehouse wall from where I dropped 7 feet inside the Warehouse and at that moment, we heard a scream outside and a sudden commotion started which made him terrified. He quickly said 'I will find and kill you if you tell this to anybody.' And tried to run away from the warehouse. He went from one door to other but all were locked until he finally found an open door on the back of the warehouse and left me, scared to death. That's when your team came inside the warehouse through the same window that I had come in and few seconds later, I heard two gunshots. That is all I know Sir. Please trust me, I am not lying.'

Rajiv got up from his seat, paced around the room, and then questioned 'Did you ever see Mr. Ghora without the mask?' Debasis answered as negative but he said he was sure it was he. Then Rajiv asked if he saw any gun on him and again Debasis answered in negative and then Rajiv asked 'How long had your discussion happened, like, how many minutes!' 'Maximum 3 to 5 minutes' answered Debasis. Finally Rajiv concluded 'Your worst enemy calls you to an empty space to kill you as he has full alibi and will never get caught, he has you in the open, he does not take your life, he does not take your money but only confesses to you about his crimes and run away! Is that what you want us to believe in?'

Debasis adjusted his seats and said 'I know it sounds weird but I swear on my daughter, this is exactly how it went through. I am not lying at all.'

Mr. Paik got up and said 'We will be the judge of that, we will verify your statement and come back to you.' He looked up to Rajiv and Mr. Dhole 'For now, let's go to the hospital and meet our hero, Akash. His operation should be over by now.'

CHAPTER 27

Rajiv, Mr. Paik and Mr. Dhole made their way to the private hospital where Akash was admitted and being treated for his injuries. He had fainted in the Warehouse site out of pain and was immediately brought to this hospital in an ambulance. The bullet had penetrated the muscles in his left shoulder and was still stuck inside when they got him to the hospital. He had to be operated for bullet wounds. No anesthesia was needed as Akash was senseless throughout the operation. Additional sedatives after the operation put him to sleep for that night and he had only regained his senses that day afternoon. He had no idea what had happened after he passed out that night but within last night and this afternoon, this case of the Green Man serial killer had taken wings and flying high towards justice and revelation. As soon as shots were fired, locals and media gathered around and news started to flow in that the serial killer, Green Man, has been caught by Detective Akash Bose with the help of the police. The fact that Akash took a bullet to his arms to stop a serial killer made Akash as much popular as a war hero. He was being cheered in every news while he was senseless. The citizens appreciated the police force's actions and every one was waiting for their hero, Akash Bose to come out safely from the hospital. The reporters were covering even miniscule updates of Akash's health and that is how Mr. Paik came to know that Akash has regained senses and made their way to the hospital. They had to cross a sea of people and reporters to reach the hospital gates as all of them asked about update on the Green Man serial killer case. They somehow managed to squeeze through with one Mantra – 'No Comments'.

Akash has no idea what the commotion outside was about but he was too sleepy to give a fuck about it. He was lying in his bed with a gloomy face but jumped up as soon as he saw Rajiv and others. He was very excited to see them and was about to get up when Mr. Paik rushed towards him and stopped him. Akash immediately started enquiring like a child 'Did he get away? Is the victim safe? Is everyone else safe? What happened there?' Rajiv cooled him down and said 'Calm down detective, calm down.'

Akash looked stunned 'Why are you calling me detective? You never do that!'

Rajiv smiled and said 'Because you have solved your first criminal case, detective, and you have got a memento of it too.' Pointing at the bullet wound on his left arm.

Akash was struggling to come to senses from the sedatives and on top of that, Rajiv's riddles only added to his problems 'We solved the case? So, we caught the Green Man? Who is he? Tell me, quickly, tell me!'

Mr. Dhole was either not confident that Rajiv was going to provide the facts this time or he was too excited about the recent developments and could not wait to share it to Akash and so he blabbered out 'The shadow you saw in the bushes was Mr. Shankar Roy, husband of Damini, the one you forged documents for! He was holding up a camera which you thought as a gun.' Mr. Dhole mentally gave a huge sigh of relief as he could finally share the juicy secret with someone. But this created a turmoil in the hospital room.

Before Akash could be surprised about these finding, Mr. Paik furiously demanded an answer from Akash 'Why did you not tell me about this thing, I thought you were clean all along and now I found out you fucked with law for a good fuck with someone's wife. This Damini or whatever that lady's name was. I thought you to be a good man but anyone who screws a married woman is an asshole and I hate that I helped you so much, you are a pure bastard Akash….you are'

Akash suddenly erupted from his bed, outraged 'Shut up Mr. Paik, shut up, what the fuck are you talking about? I did not sleep with Damini, I loved her, I loved her because she was in so much pain. She used her pain as a weapon to manipulate me and melt me. I did help her and forged documents for her but I did it only because she told me that she was raped and tortured by her husband every night. I even was an eyewitness to such a torture when I filmed the video. I had no clue what she did to provoke her husband to hit her; all I saw was somebody in pain, getting tortured. All I wanted was to love her and save her from that kind of physical abuse every night and so, I helped her in all ways I could. I did not sleep with her as I am not a jerk or desperate. You may think whatever you want but I do not think I did anything wrong. Even if I did, my intentions were right and I would do it over again, if the reasons are right.'

Rajiv was surprised at this sudden outburst. 'So, you did not cheat on Shankar, he is after your neck all this while and having nightmares about you and Damini for nothing!' Rajiv sounded happily surprised.

Akash's voice had some regret and compassion 'If he had to go after someone's neck, he should have gone for Samir's because he is the one who fucked Damini and betrayed her. Too late........ things would

have been so different if he had chosen his target more thoughtfully.'

Rajiv noticed a spark in Akash's eyes and said 'Why too late and what would have been different?'

Akash said with regret 'If he was not there in the shadows, then I would not have ruined the original plan and improvised, ending up getting shot and shooting someone, wait, Rajiv....... Whom did I shoot?

How is he now? Is he the Green Man? I am not able to sleep thinking that I have shot someone. It has morally killed me. He is alive right?'

Rajiv paused for a brief and said 'What you did was to stop a criminal, running from law. Very few could do that, especially after being shot.'

Akash interrupted 'Yes I know but it is not helping me from the inside. I had never ever thought that it would come to it. I just cannot sleep thinking that I could have killed someone. I will never be able to justify this to myself, never.'

Rajiv again paused before he spoke. He made eye contact with the others in the room and all of them agreed over eye contact. 'We have got the Green Man, which is what matters Akash.'

Akash was about to get up from his bed 'What do you mean that we have got him? Did I hit him? Did I kill him? Oh my God, no no, fuck man, fuck!'

Mr. Paik came closer to console Akash 'No young man, you did shoot at him when he was climbing the wall. It did not hit him but it scared him so much that his foot slipped and he fell down.' Mr. Paik looked up to everyone and everyone agreed to commit the sin of lying.

Akash looked a lot relaxed now and said 'So I did not hit him! Really! Wow! But how did we get him then?'

Mr. Paik sat down in the bed and continued swimming in sins 'This distraction gave our officers enough time to close the gap between the Green Man and them. Once Green Man was on top of the wall again, about to jump to the other side, our officer fired at him. It hit his back and instead of jumping down, he fell face first on the other side. We took him to the hospital but he was Blue and lifeless by then.'

A ray of happiness flashed through Akash 'So, he is dead! I must be a pig as I am actually happy that it is over.'

Mr. Dhole said 'We all are pigs in that aspect.' and gave a porky laugh.

Akash now looked at everyone with expectant eye 'Who is he?'

As usual, the final blow has to be by Mr. Dhole so that the butterflies in his stomach can take some rest 'Mr. Ashish Ghora.'

Everyone expected Akash to be shouting in surprise but Akash kept quite as if he was analysing all the findings until now and connecting all the dots. Finally, he spoke 'So, he put someone else's body in the car? But we had the CCTV footage! Ok, he placed the body after he crossed the toll. So, whose body was it in the car?'

Rajiv helped 'Wow! Full marks for your reaction Detective. You showed real composure there. Bikram Pal, the man who was Mr. Ghora's right hand and betrayed him. He had killed him before he staged the car accident. He got his revenge too with this plot. He had called his arch-rival Mr. Debasis Sen to Rhino Warehouse that night to do a full circle of revenges and then, vanish in thin air as he is already pronounced dead. A perfect plan.'

Akash said 'Did he do all of this to avoid life sentence?'

Mr. Paik gave a smirk and said 'And he got a lifeless sentence in return, thanks to you Akash.'

'Please Mr. Paik, I did not do anything, I apologize to have ruined your plan that night as I really thought that the shadow was holding a gun that night towards Rajiv.'

Rajiv laughed and said 'It's a logical mistake that can happen to anyone. Thanks a lot son, for saving me from that one as I am as much afraid of a camera, as I am of a gun. The former can do me more harm.'

Now it was Mr. Dhole's turn to be a smirk 'But your family does not get any insurance claim for the damage caused by a camera, Ha Ha Ha.' No one laughed but it did not budge him.

Akash was still calculating all the facts 'So, he killed Mr. Khan to set a trend, planted the Green Man story, put the first letter in my flat and acted as the second victim. He was about to kill the third when we stopped him. So, all of his enemies would be dead and he would have escaped his life imprisonment!'

Mr. Paik said 'I cannot believe how much selfish people can be and to what extent they will go for personal gains.'

Akash said 'If he had called Mr. Khan to the sweet shop, why did Mr. Khan write 'A.D' in his diary note!'

Mr. Dhole said 'May be he was not referring to his surname in the diary. I often store numbers in my phone as the name of the person followed by a word by which I can refer to the man like I have Kanchan Keymaker, Rudra Rickshaw, Palash Bannerghata, this makes it easier to refer to the person. Ashish Ghora ran a company for Dyes, Chemicals named Ashish Dyes Co. and he lived in Dhakuria, Kolkata. So maybe that is what Mr. Khan was referring to Ashish Dyes or Ashish Dhakuria!'

Everyone looked stunned at Mr. Dhole. Rajiv looked at Mr. Dhole as he had never looked at him before. He had never spoken smart words but we live in a world of exceptions, Akash finally opened up with congratulations and others followed. Rajiv concluded the congratulations by saying 'Well done Mr. Dhole. That is indeed a good explanation. Therefore, I think we are covered from every points now. The case is closed and we have brought a criminal to God's justice. Well done everyone. We are having a party once Akash is out of here in a weeks' time. Then we will have the formal press conference with our hero here.' He smashed his fist to Akash's shoulders in appreciation. Akash just smiled and said 'Do I get any fees for what we have achieved? I am not salaried like you guys as you already know.'

Mr. Paik said 'We can arrange for that, young man, we surely can. Congratulations in wrapping up your first criminal case. You have a very bright career ahead, Detective.'

CHAPTER 28

Finally, the challenger, the underdog, the common man, has done what even police could not do. He has brought a killer to justice and saved the society. This was the trend of the stories doing rounds in internet and TV. The public adored their new hero and the news channels continuously ran news on Akash's health recovery for the next five days. People from everywhere sent good wishes and as Akash was still few hospital doors away from the camera, the media diverted their attention to Akash's family. When Akash left his comfortable high package job for the trivial purpose of following his dream and attempt to be a successful private detective, Akash's father could not handle the disappointment from his own blood and the depression caused by it slowly and slowly deteriorated his health. When Akash got caught at forging documents in court and it was broadcasted everywhere, the disgrace caused by it hammered the last nail in the coffin and soon, Akash's father succumbed to fate and closed his eyes forever.

When his father had died, Akash was under arrest for lying in court and could not even come to his own father's funeral for performing last rights. Since then, his family members had broken ties with him. They never used to contact him. Akash's mother could never forgive his son for disappointing his father but her motherly instinct would not let her completely void all contacts with his son and so she rarely called up his son to check upon him but their relation was hanging by a thread. She would check upon Akash every fortnight. Akash was going through a lot of emotional turmoil, was fed up of his lonely life, and was always looking to speak more often with his mother but she refused to respond equally. Although she acted strict over the phone but she could emotionally never let go off her son. She

regularly checked every news that came out about the Green Man and always had the news channels turned on. She even stopped watching her favorite soap series as she could not surf away from news channels to get any kind of news about her beloved son.

Akash was due to be released from hospital the next day. Lately, a habit has been forced on to him, the reporters would approach his mother and other relatives and they would pour sweet words about him for the black box. He would switch on the TV in his hospital room throughout the day and surf for such news. Mr. Paik had thrown a party in his home in the honor of Akash, the day Akash was due to be released. Akash had plans to go to his home immediately after release but a press conference was scheduled for the next day and so he agreed to go to Mr. Paik's home that day and finish the conference the next day, then take a long leave from work, and go back to home. Mr. Paik had also a gift in store for him, which would be felicitated, in his house party, which was another reason for Akash to stay. A while back, Akash had requested to be monetarily rewarded for his actions that night. Though Mr. Paik had a hard time to arrange for the same from the police force, he had played around well about that piece of work and manipulated a local municipal authority to award Akash with a hefty sum for his bravery in the presence of media. The municipal authority obviously did it for the 60 seconds of fame but no one cared about that. So, on release from the hospital, he escaped the media via the back gate and was escorted to Mr. Paik's home for the night.

As Akash entered Mr. Paik's home, he was greeted with applauds by everyone in the room. Akash embarrassingly smiled and said 'Was this really necessary? Thanks a lot everyone but I think we should clap for every police officer involved with the case, specially, Mr. Paik, Mr. Dhole and Rajiv, a huge round of applauds to them too please' and he started a chain of claps which lasted for fewer seconds than his turn. After the initial formalities were over, Akash was invited to a corner where the local municipal authority bestowed a flower bouquet to him. Akash wondered why a flower bouquet when he was expecting Gandhi ji pictures but his grudge soon subsided as he landed eyes on an envelope inside the bouquet. The pictures captured only the bouquet but Akash cared less about that, he quickly went to the washroom, opened the envelope and was rightly greeted with a cheque. Looking at the sum, he gave away a breath of pleasure. Finally something to fill in his bank account. He gave a shy of relief, looked into his reflection in the mirror, smiled to himself, straightened his jacket and made his way out to the room. But the felicitations were not over yet. As the party kicked in with drinks and snacks, Rajiv tinged a toast, raised his glasses, and said 'I must say, I underestimated this lad but he never stopped to surprise me. To go up against a serial killer with no combat training and only courage at heart itself speaks volumes about him. In the Warehouse, there was a situation where he said to us that he needs a gun to defend his life and he honored that gun by bringing down the Green Man. I am a simple public servant and I am not rich enough to give him many gifts but there is one gift I can give him now. While he was hospitalized, I discussed with the commissioner and got a gun license for him as he indeed deserves the honor to carry one and act for justice in coming days too. So, Detective Akash Bose, if you can come forward please'

Akash looked quite confused but obeyed.

Rajiv brought out a police belt with rifle holder and the holder was glorified with an operational rifle. Akash stood there astonished. Everyone in the room clapped. Rajiv laid an encouraging hand in Akash's shoulder and asked him to wear it. Akash obliged again and stood there dumb struck. Rajiv said 'Don't worry, its licensed to you and you completely deserve this honor. I hope you use it for the right reasons henceforth.'

As the night moved on, the crowd eased on to their home too until Rajiv, Mr. Paik and Mr. Dhole were the only company available to Akash. They went to the balcony with their glasses and lighted a smoke. Mr. Paik said 'Rajiv, I did not know about the gun, how you convinced the commissioner for it?'

Rajiv laughed and said 'I told him that Akash can be jailed to fire at someone without a gun license.'

Akash said 'Is it true!'

Mr. Paik smiled and said 'Well, technically, yes, but I think we are far away from that and there is always the ground of self-defense.'

Mr. Dhole interrupted 'But, Akash, how does it feel to get shot?'

Akash said 'I would have known better if I had my senses but it was terribly painful.'

Mr. Dhole was not satisfied yet 'You know if I was there that night and if I had taken the bullet, I would have got promoted by now. Does it hurt much?'

Rajiv joked 'How about I arrange for your promotion? I can ask one of the gangs to give you a shot, is that fine?' everyone busted out laughing except the man dreaming of a promotion.

As the soft talks had eased the mood, Rajiv landed the blow 'Akash, now that you are physically and mentally fit, let me tell you a truth. Please don't react to this. You really did the right thing.'

Akash straightened 'What do you mean Rajiv?'

Rajiv said 'Lad, while you were down from the gunshot, you managed to fire a shot at the Green Man, Ashish Ghora.'

Akash just responded with a curious 'Yeah!'

Rajiv continued 'Your shot hit Mr. Ashish Ghora in the left side of the belly and he fell down. We took him to the hospital but before he could be treated, he was pronounced dead.'

Akash fell from the sky 'You mean I killed him! Oh shit, I really killed him! My god My god how can I do that. Trust me everyone I had no clue, Oh shit oh shit how could I do this, I have no clue, why the fuck did I fire…'

Mr. Paik quickly got hold of him and shaked him to bring him out of the trance. He held him firm and said 'Look at me Akash, you did the right thing. You caught him. Otherwise, he would have fled the law and could be never found again. You did the exact right thing. You have to accept it as a great deed of courage. You did nothing wrong.'

Akash shrugged himself from the strong grip and said 'How can you call this as the right thing? He could not see another morning because of me. I have no right to take someone's life. That is never justified. Not at my level. Just for my foolish act, his family would never see him. How can I ever justify this to myself!'

Rajiv took his turn 'Dude, he was already dead to everyone. He was killing people like they were mosquitos. If you hadn't stopped him, he would have gone on to kill 10 more. You stopped him from taking further lives. I know how you are feeling as I felt the exact same way when I had to shoot at my first encounter. I could not sleep for a fortnight but I had the same consolation as you. If I did not kill him, he would go ahead and kill 10 more. You have stopped that from happening. That is a hero's act. You should be proud of saving the society from him.'

Akash gulped his drinks and said 'You are a police officer Rajiv, you get training for this and this is in your job description.'

Rajiv said 'I can lecture you a lot about what you said but I would rather stay silent so that I can enjoy my drink. You did a good job lad, live with it. Anyways, you need to prepare for tomorrow. You did all right in the warehouse. That will be your legacy and tomorrow everyone is going to know about your legacy.'

Akash calmed down a bit and the fears of the press conference took over him. He said 'They don't know!'

Mr. Paik said 'They will tomorrow. Akash, the real test is tomorrow. We have the press conference. Are you ready? The press wants to hear it from their hero only.'

Akash said 'I have not been this terrified before going to the warehouse too. What will they ask me? What should I say?'

Rajiv rudely said ''Us'. They will ask 'Us'. We are also part of the story you know.'

Akash said 'I did not mean it that way Rajiv. I am just nervous about tomorrow'

Rajiv did not stop 'So am I dear, so am I.'

CHAPTER 29

The police force had arranged for a press conference for the final revelations about the Green man case. Reporters from all around the nation had gathered in the massive hall to celebrate the victory of Akash over the Green Man. As the police had maintained total anonymity for all this time about the Green Man's identity, the excitement and suspense, around it was no less that the suspense of 'Katappa ne Bahubali ko kiu mara?' Finally the day had come when all that had transpired for all this time would be detailed to everyone by their very own hero, Akash Bose. Even Akash's mother and other family members had come to the press conference. Everyone out there was guessing who can be the devil's face behind the Green Man. This guessing game had been going on for all this week and it was about time to put everyone's guessing power to the test. Akash's family were given VIP seats and the stage was set for Akash to disclose the series of events, which led to the capture and demise of the Green Man.

A loud cheer erupted through the hall as Akash and Rajiv and Mr. Paik entered the Dias and took their seat. Everyone was chanting slogans in the name of Akash only. Rajiv felt irritated to see all their effort

go to Akash's pocket just because a bullet hit him. He said 'I feel like a havildar with Commissioner Akash Bose taking all the credit.' Akash understood the frustration and said that he will do all he can to show to everyone how much the police force had worked hard to solve this case. As the police officers calmed everyone down, Akash started to explain. 'Hi Everyone, thanks a lot for your support throughout this case and especially after I was admitted to the hospital. I would like to thank everyone who wished me well. Apart from all the things that happened during the course of this case, I am most happy about the fact that my Mom is here, in front of me, with a proud heart and tears in her eyes. I have always shed her tears for the wrong reasons and so, now, I feel like I have finally lived up to her expectation. It melts my heart to see that she is here by my side. For those of you who do not know this, when I left my corporate job to follow my dream of becoming a private detective, my parents had to face a lot of spat from neighbors and relatives and they could not support my decision as it was not a positive step for my career. Still I pursued my dream but while doing so, I had let my family down, I had hardly talked to my Mom open heartedly for months and I hugely miss it. I partly hold myself responsible for my father's depression, which ultimately took away my lifelong hero from me. I wish my father would be here, now, by my mother's side and I am sure he would also have the same tears in his eyes as my Mom. Thanks you Mom for being their always by my side and I would like to apologize to you in front of everyone for everything I couldn't be, which you wanted me to be. I had acted selfish but I just could not have continued with the corporate life.'

By now, Akash's voice was wet and he needed some time away from the mic to clear the tears of his eyes. The media focussed their lenses on Akash's mother who looked like an angel, crying in peace. She extended her hands from the seat to symbolically, bless her son. Soon Akash resumed speaking 'Before we start with the details, it is mandatory for all of you to note that I played a trivial part in this case and the maximum work was done by the respected police officers who are sitting alongside me. Rajiv, Mr. Dhole and Mr. Paik were the backbone of this operation and were the mastermind to catch the Green Man.'

The crowd did not seem convinced and did not look to be in any mood to appreciate the police force. The cat and mouse relation between them did not help to lend an open ear to the police force's praise. 'Everyone knows about the first murder by the Green Man. I somehow got involved in that case and though I never wanted it, I was branded as the challenger to the Green Man. You, the media, owes me an apology for that one as without making a single challenge to the Green Man, I became his challenger and his playmate in this wicked game of blood. While the police force was still helping me to gather further evidences from Mr. Khan's murder, I received a letter from the Green Man. The letter would be shared with you. It was a riddle, which the police force helped me to debug. After toiling at it for a day, we could finally figure out that the next target is Mr. Ashish Ghora from Kolkata. The businessman, who was soon to be sentenced and punished by the High Court for dumping waste chemicals in the water which prompted a flood in a village in West Bengal.'

As Akash took a break, everyone in the room waited for him to catch up on his breath and resume. 'We were not aware at this point of time that we were actually being followed. We only came to know about this during our last encounter with the Green Man in Rhino Warehouse. I will spare you the suspense and let you know that we were being followed by your pal, Ex media reporter, Mr. Shankar Roy.'

An awe passed through the whole room. Among many of the reporters waiting for their chance to speak, one of them pounced on the opportunity and got up and asked from the stands 'Is it the same

Shankar Roy against whom you had provided false evidence?' Akash reduced his voice, sulked, and answered in affirmative. Questions were coming from all around now 'Is he the Green Man?' 'How was he involved in this?' 'Was he taking revenge on you?' 'Was he following you?' 'How did he get to know of the riddle and Mr. Ghora?' All of this questions banged Akash's eardrums at the same time. Every reporter got up and started to put forward a new question.

Akash had never faced this and he just stared blankly from one face to another, following the source of the questions, which he could hear. Mr. Paik stood up and said 'If you ask 100 questions, you will get no answers. If you ask 10 questions, you will get 10 answers. Your choice. Everyone paused. Mr. Paik was not finished 'I would answer few questions which I could register. Shankar had bugged Akash's house with a hidden speaker and when we were decoding the riddle, he overheard everything. The Green Man had secretly tipped Mr. Shankar about the first murder and that is how Mr. Shankar got involved in this. This has got nothing to do with Akash, the Green Man found Shankar as an easy picking as he was not having any reporting job presently and would be unable to trace Green Man's number. If that is all, can we proceed?'

A few seconds of silence in a room full of reporters is rare and Akash respected it by breaking it. 'We went to Mr. Ghora's home in Kolkata to discuss the issue. Shankar was already present there in the disguise of a gardener and ran away when we arrived. We did not know it was Shankar back then but later on, he confessed about this. He was there to gather further information about Mr. Ghora. Mr. Ghora was not available in his home and so, we had a discussion with his family. Mr. Ghora was supposed to meet us in the police station next day. Unfortunately, as you all know, he died in a car crash that night which we supposed that the Green Man masterminded and killed his target. The body was too much burnt to be identified but we found Mr. Ghora's belongings in the car and the body.'

A second of pause and the reporters pounced on their chance to ask few questions 'Do you mean the Green man did not kill Mr. Ghora?' 'Why could not you catch Shankar at Mr. Ghora's home?' 'What are your investigation on the crash?' 'Who was the Green Man?'

Just like the monitor of a class, Rajiv stood up and said 'Do you want to hear about how we got to know of things we presently know? Or, do you want us to tell you, in a short and crisp way, what we know presently?'

No one from the media answered and Rajiv assumed the silence to be in his favor and urged Akash to continue as he sat down.

Akash obeyed 'As we got busy with the investigation, two days followed and we received another letter, another riddle from the Green Man. Like last time, we toiled for hours and hours and ultimately found out that the riddle solves to Rhino Warehouse in China Town at 22:10 pm on the full moon night, which was that night itself. That is where the Green Man would kill his next victim. So, Mr. Paik and Rajiv prepared our plan to catch the Green Man and we reached the site well before time. The plan was to guard all exit points from the warehouse and Rajiv and Mr. Paik would go in to arrest the Green Man alive. As I had no combat or stealth experience, I was supposed to be inside the boundary of the compound but away from the actual warehouse structure where any action can happen. I would be their extra eyes and ears and inform them anything that I can see. I was strictly informed by Mr. Paik and Rajiv, not to get involved in any fighting but for personal safety, I was given a gun, for worst case scenarios.'

Everyone started questioning again 'A gun! How can you give a gun to someone who does not have any license to use it?' 'So, did the Green Man come to the Warehouse, did he shoot you?' 'What was in the letter?'

Akash continued 'May be if we proceed further and complete describing what happened, then we can entertain questions? I was standing at the corner of the boundary and Mr. Paik's force was slowly and stealthily moving towards the warehouse. The Green Man was already inside with his target. We later on came to know that his target, who was inside the warehouse was Kolkata's famous businessman Debasis Sen.

'As the team was moving in, suddenly I saw a movement in the darkness opposite me. I looked into the darkness carefully and saw a silhouette of an image in the darkness, holding something shiny and moving towards Rajiv and others. As I stressed more, I could see a shiny dark object, rising up and pointing towards Rajiv. I was sure it was a gun and I thought that this was a trap and the Green Man was actually in the darkness, moments away from shooting down our team. Rajiv and others had no clue about this as the shadow was coming from their rear. I tried to inform them but my voice choked. It was a first time for me, that so many emotions had strangled me, my heart was beating louder than a drum and I tried harder to speak up but could not. At that point of time, I did not have any clue what I am doing, whether it is right or wrong but I just could not be a spectator of a massacre and so I started running towards the shadow to save our team. As I started running, I found my voice back but by that time, I was so excited and I was trying so hard to speak out all this time, I roared instead of whisper, as I should have. This had saved our team as the man in the darkness got scared and ran out from the warehouse, without shooting. Our team scrambled and few officers went to chase the shadow. By then, our stealth was over and we were outnumbered. The Green Man would defintely know that we were there and would surely kill his victim and make a run for it now and so we had to quickly run each towards one exit gate to stop him. My luck had never been my lady and this was no exception, the Green Man had to exit by the gate I went to cover. Just as he saw me, he shot at me and it hit my shoulders. I fell down but something in me just could not see this story end like this. I could not let a killer get away from me when he is so close to me. Lying in the ground, I gathered all my strengths to put some kind on aim and then, I fired a shot. After that I collapsed and passed out. Later on, I came to know that the shadow I saw was Shankar, pointing his camera to get a shot of the action, my shot had pierced Green Man's belly, and he could not make it to the hospital alive. I had taken a life and I can never forgive myself for this.'

From the experience of the last 10 minutes, a moment of silence by Akash would be greeted with ~5 questions from the reporters but this time, most of them nodded their heads in appreciation. Two of the reporters stayed loyal to their profession and asked the odd questions 'How could you aim after being shot!' 'Who is the Green Man?'

Akash responded 'I don't know, I really don't know how I managed to shoot. I have been lying in my hospital bed for the last 7 days, unable to get out of my bed because I was shot but how could I raise my arms and shoot after getting shot, I have no idea. Will power I guess or adrenaline burst. It shocks me too!'

Everyone jerked their faces in appreciation and Akash's mother could not control her tears still. Her heart would have stopped beating if anything had happened to Akash.

Akash then said 'Rajiv was much focused to save the victim and he successfully saved Mr. Sen from the clutches of the Green Man. And now, the time to reveal the identity of the Green Man, here it goes. It was Mr. Ashish Ghora'

A loud sound of awe travelled to the room, reporters got busy calling or texting or writing while others showered the Dias members with questions.

Mr. Paik stepped in now, 'Instead of answering your questions one by one, please let us tell you our findings and then all of your questions should get automatically answered. Mr. Ghora was due to be sentenced for life imprisonment as his company had polluted River Ganges, which caused a flood in a village by the banks of the river. He knew that the sentence was going to be life imprisonment. So, he thought of this crooked plan. He setup a story about a serial killer killing businessmen who were not responsible towards mother nature. The same thing for which he was guilty, so that he can also be considered as the serial killer's victim without anyone doubting about it. First, he killed Mr. Khan to spread the news. He had read about Shankar's divorce case and chose Shankar as he had no hands on any active media technologies to back trace to Mr. Ghora. Somehow, Akash got involved in this case and you people started to call him a challenger. Mr. Ghora had the perfect background now. He had staged a serial killer case and lured the media to it. So, the police will be more focused on catching the serial killer than treating this as homicide and digging deep into the case. He planted the letter in Akash's room, to which he has confessed too. When her wife informed him that we had come to meet with him, he was sure that we have understood his hint in the letter and now was the time for his act. He had a rival from the past who is physically of the same build as him and so, he invited Mr. Bikram Pal to go to Digha with him to which Bikram happily agreed. Mr. Ashish Ghora slipped some sleeping pill into Bikram Pal's drink and then killed Bikram in his sleep by smashing his head with a rock. He has confessed of this to Mr. Debasis Sen. Then he placed his documents on Bikram's body and burnt the car. It looked like the Green Man had killed Mr. Ghora, just as he wanted. The whole line of investigation turned to the Green man instead of him. Though both were same, he was the Green man but it diverted the police's attention away from the case. He still had one enemy left in this world. His age-old rival, Debasis Sen. Green Man was the perfect excuse to murder him too and hence he wrote another letter to us, this time hinting on the location, so that we can be witnesses and we again blame this murder on the Green Man while he roams free. May be he planned to leave the country after this but that remains unknown. That is all about the Green man that we know of. He had already confessed his crimes to Mr. Debasis Sen and God has punished him accordingly. A round of applauds for Akash please, who made it happen.'

CHAPTER 30

A bunch of questions followed to drill down to the tits and bits of the issue and this was already flashing everywhere in the news. The media was shocked that Mr. Ghora was the serial killer but disappointed too that it was fake, there was no environment factor that everyone appreciated with the serial killers intentions, the serial killer was just a made up stage so that Mr. Ghora could take his revenges and save himself from going to prison. The media was not satisfied still. They were very happy with Akash but they were yet not satisfied as they had expected a huge revelation and it had not lived up to the craze. So, they thought of finding a new pointer to this story. The inefficiency of the police to do something which eventually, a common man had to do. They started to question Mr. Paik first and then moved on to Rajiv 'Why were police not able to catch the Green Man, may be then he could have been caught alive!'

Mr. Paik calmly said 'If everything went according to plan and Akash had not blown our cover by shouting, that is exactly what would have happened.'

Another reporter said 'But why did you take Akash to a critical mission as this? Though I praise the lord, that you did take Akash with you otherwise the killer would still be roaming free now.'

Mr. Paik was not calm anymore but still maintained composure to say 'Akash was part of this team and we had asked Akash to sit this one out but Akash would not listen. Hence we had him sit at a corner, not take part in any actions.'

'How can you give a gun to just anyone! Isn't that against the law?'

Fuck calmness, Mr. Paik stood up from his seat and roared this time 'So what do you think we should have done, leave him empty handed so that if the Green Man runs into him, he can only fold his hands and apologize! We had repeatedly told Akash, not to use the revolver unless absolutely necessary and I stand proud here, as I gave him the revolver or else he would be dead by now!'

Having already got some juicy reactions to feed the TV screen for a day from Mr. Paik, the reporters now took their chance with Rajiv. They turned towards him and said 'What were you doing all this time Sir, you are one of the brightest police officers of our country, everyone knows that and still you could do nothing, even after receiving the letters! How could you get fooled by a 50 year old!'

Rajiv responded sharply 'My main focus was to save the third victim which we did'

A reporter spanked back 'But what about all this while when Mr. Ghora was fooling around with the whole police force, what were you doing Sir and what are your contributions to solve this case.

Rajiv looked around the room. Akash and Mr. Paik had supporting gaze but the reporters demanded him to speak and so he did 'I was thinking. I was thinking a lot in the last seven days'

'The case got solved 8 days ago and you were only thinking for the last 7 days! We wanted to know what you did during the case, when it really mattered. What's the use of thinking about the case when the case is solved.'

Rajiv said 'I was thinking because somethings did not fit, they just did not fit.'

Media countered immediately 'What do you mean?'

Rajiv was still in his calm self and said 'Have any of you in this room played the tougher levels of Sudoku?'

Everyone paused and was about to question further but by then, Rajiv had restarted 'In the tough levels of Sudoku, there occasionally comes a point where you do not have a next move. You have no numbers fitting any box with 100% surety. All of the empty boxes can hold more than one probable numbers.

That is the time when you have to find a box, which has only two possible answers, and guess one. Then you put all the subsequent numbers, which are deduced from your guess number in small markings as they might need to be changed again if your guess was wrong. If everything fits in, then your guess was right and if any box does not fit in, then you are sure about what your guessing box must contain and you correct it and progress again.'

'What has this to do with this case!' asked a journalist.

'From the start of the case, I felt and even expressed multiple times to Akash that the letters that the Green Man is sending is not the style of a serial killer. A serial killer's letter will reveal the exact same information every time. Here, for the first murder, there was no letters sent to anyone, for the second, it gave away only the victim's name and the third gave away only the time and place of the killing. This is not a serial killer's rule and a serial killers rule is unbreakable. So, I had always assumed that we were not dealing with a psycho, obsessed with saving the planet. It was as if I was in that Sudoku board and my guess was that Mr. Ghora was the serial killer. I did not need to guess, he had already confessed to be the serial killer but my numbers were still not matching. My Sudoku board still conflicted; I could not be 100% sure if this is right, that, Mr. Ashish Ghora is the Green Man.'

'What kind of conflicts?' Akash asked instead of the media.

'Akash, put yourself in Mr. Ghora's shoes and think for a moment. If you had to create a news about a serial killer out loose, why do it in Bangalore whereas you plan to kill yourself as the next victim in Kolkata! I mean what are the chances that a serial killer's rumor, only after the first murder would be of a national interest and he can use the same story for killing himself in Kolkata! What if this story did not go viral and spread like a wild fire, what if it flashed in Bangalore news only and the fear did not reach Kolkata? If you were to create that story of a serial killer, why would you try your luck with killing someone in Bangalore and wait for it to be a national news? Why would you not kill a reputed business man in Kolkata itself! That way, his next plot of killing himself matches the location of the serial killer and he can easily get away with it. Isn't that right?'

There was a murmur of agreement in the hall.

'Secondly, if you are to stage a serial killer story, before the murder, why not send a note to the media or the police station or an anonymous post in Facebook or anything else which would feed the headlines already before the kill or even after. The way things happened in reality, the story of the Green Man would never had reached the news if a police officer found the letter in Mr. Khan's body. He would have given the letter to his supervisor and the police would have taken up this case internally, not in the limelight of the whole Indian citizens. The story reached media only because Akash had found the letter and shouted in front of the reporters about the Green Man!

Akash bowed his head down in apology but Rajiv was in no mood to stop. 'So, what does not match in the Sudoku board is that why Mr. Ghora chose Bangalore instead of Kolkata and why did he not advertise the serial killer story before the first murder? Another thing that does not fit in, are the information in the letter. Mr. Ghora may be a common man but should already know from Bollywood and Hollywood movies and books that serial killers follow a pattern and he needs to pass the same type of information if he has to stage the serial killer story correctly. But he did not. The letters have no

pattern; one is written on a tissue paper, and the next two on a typewriter or a computer printout. As I previously said, the information on the letters are also different in each occasion.'

'Then again, if we are to assume the age factor of Mr. Ghora and after all he has been through, assume that he was not particularly gifted beneath the skull, can you explain me this! Why did he not kill his archrival, Debasis Sen even when he had a gun? He definitely did not call him to the

Rhino Warehouse to chat and confess about this crimes but that is exactly what he did! He just chatted with him and bragged about himself. This man was sick enough to smash a sleeping man's face with rock until it iwas unrecognizable. So, we cannot assume that he was too soft hearted to kill Debasis. Even when he got to know about our presence and he knows that Debasis knows everything now and can leak those secrets to police, why did he not kill him! He had a gun and he was close enough to him to lay a head shot but no such thing happened. He even did not take the one crore rupees which Debasis had brought with him. A man on the run, one crore rupees can be a game changer, but again, he did not do that! Why!'

Akash said 'May be he could not act at that point of time when the rush began, I mean when I freaked out and shouted to reveal our presence. May be, initially, he thought that he has enough time to kill him. You know how a person's stomach wiggle till they boast about their achievements!'

Rajiv again continued 'But what about your achievements Akash, shooting someone after being hit with a bullet! Kudos to you man. You are really a star. I had to train 5 years with guns to hit a target. Initially, in all my senses, I could only manage to be meters away from the whole target figure, leave alone the bull's eye. But you could hit Mr. Ghora fatally even after being hit by a bullet and when you are about to lose your senses. Hats off to you lad but your fingers should have been numb at that time and still you managed to pull the trigger. But coming to my Sudoku board, that was the last thing that was not matching, how can a rookie get hit by a bullet and still hit someone exactly at a point in the belly where it would be fatal and the most interesting point to be considered is that this was the first shot of your life! Wasn't it?'

Akash shied away and said 'It was just a lucky shot. I did not know how it happened but it must be plain reflex to the shock of getting shot and the Green Man getting away.'

Rajiv said 'Yes, probable but still that's highly improbable.'

Seing someone harassing their hero and that too in front of the hero's mother did not sit well with the reporters and they immediately reciprocated 'So, Mr. Rajiv, our super cop, why are you having doubts when Mr. Ashish Ghora has confessed about it himself and what grand steps did you take about your doubts?'

Rajiv turned towards the media 'I started out to do the basics first. I thought that Mr. Khan must have been another of Mr. Ghora's enemy from the past and hence he choose Bangalore as his first murder location. I could not find of a better explanation. I did a full background check of Mr. Khan and then.......I hit jackpot.'

Akash looked worried now. The reporters did not wait for a pause from Rajiv, but made the pause happen. They interrupted Rajiv with a shower of questions mostly around what he was referring to as the jackpot. Had they not questioned, may be they would have received the answer quicker but human behaviors are guided by habits and media have the habit of questioning. Rajiv resumed 'To answer your questions, NO, Mr. Khan was not related to Mr. Ghora by any means.'

The crowd was pissed now 'So, why are you calling it a Jackpot!'

Rajiv looked at Akash and Akash appeared to be pleading to Rajiv with his eyes but Rajiv ignored it. 'Mr. Khan, or Mr. Samir Khan, who was the first victim of the Green Man was actually the same person with whom Mrs. Damini Roy had the extra marital affair with. You remember Mrs. Damini Roy? The same lady for whom, Akash had forged documents in court against Shankar.'

Chapter 31

Akash still did not utter a single word. Everyone looked surprised, especially Akash and his mother. Mr. Paik questioned before the media 'So, this is also related to Akash! Just like Shankar?' He turned his gaze to Akash and said 'Akash, did you know that Mr. Khan was Damini's boyfriend? Did you meet him before or know who he was?'

Akash was about to answer but Rajiv stole his chance 'I had been thinking of the same thing and now it made sense. Do you remember Mr. Paik, in the hospital room, when we were discussing about Shankar's rage on Akash and Akash mentioned that it should have been channeled on Samir instead of Akash as Samir had slept with Damini and ruined Shankar's life?' Mr. Paik nodded affirmatively and Rajiv continued 'Akash had said then that it is too late now to channel that rage on Samir. Now those lines make sense as he knew well enough that Mr. Khan is Samir and he is dead now.'

Akash shouted in his defense 'What are you saying! I did not know that Mr. Khan is Damini's Ex. It is news for me too and I am equally surprised. Are you sure of this Rajiv? I had said that it's too late as the damage on myself had already been done. I am scared for life for shooting someone dead. I have blood on my hand because of Shankar and I meant that it is too late to fix it now. He has already screwed my life. Why won't you ever believe that I am innocent?'

Rajiv defended himself 'I am not putting anything on you Akash, yet. The reporter here asked me what I had done for this case and I am just answering them.' Then he faced the reporters again and continued while Akash still gazed at him in awe 'Now I thought to myself, who has the most convincing reasons to kill Mr. Samir Khan except Mr. Ashish Ghora. I went to Mr. Khan's house to investigate further. There was not much money left to anyone in particular after his death. Everyone loved him and his wife did not know anything about Damini, at least that's what I could make out. Though there were no specific reasons for me to doubt

Mr. Khan's family, just for investigation's sake, I still considered them. So my suspect list now were Ashish, Shankar, Akash, Damini and Mr. Khan's family.'

Rajiv took a pause but no one interrupted him 'We have already discussed about Ashish. Mr. Khan's family had no motive, as there was not much money involved in it. One factor could have been that Mrs. Haseena Khan had come to know about Damini Roy and killed her husband in revenge. So, I could not rule her out totally yet. Damini was out of the country and so, she could be ruled out. Shankar had a very positive motive to kill Mr. Khan but he did not know of his identity. I had interrogated Shankar again about his whereabouts for a week to the day Mr. Khan was killed, his stories match with his phone tower location. But I did not completely rule him out of the case yet. I mean he was very much involved in spreading the Green Man news and may be, he had personal gains from that. So, he still stands as a strong suspect. Then we come to our hero, Akash Bose' and he turned to Akash and continued 'Let's consider Akash that you had heard of Samir's name only once during Damini's confession but you are a private detective. It's your job to find out identities and hence you were successfully able to track that Samir is Mr. Khan.' Akash was about to interrupt but Rajiv just raised a hand and continued 'Now, it is quite logical that you were very angry at that time with Damini but she was not reachable anymore. She was in another country. So, you could have diverted your anger to Samir. You loved Damini and you knew that Samir had unlawfully had a sexual relationship with Damini and he betrayed her as he never told her that he is married too. If Damini knew that Samir was married then the divorce case would never have happened and you would never have met Damini. Your life would have been so perfect. That kept on revolving in your head and when you tailed Mr. Samir Khan and saw his face for the first time, may be, you were not able to sleep at nights as you could see Damini making passionate love with Samir whenever you closed your eyes, just as Shankar dreams about you and Damini'

'What are you saying Rajiv! Why would I do that? Yes I did fall for Damini but I am not a psycho!'

Rajiv only said 'Akash, this are all my assumptions, please do not take it personally. I am just filling in my Sudoku board with all the options and proper reasons to it.'

Rajiv continued again 'There were too many suspects, I needed to filter more and so, I thought about inspecting the leftovers from Mr. Khan's body that was under police custody. As this case was treated as a serial killer's victim and not as a homicide, I did not look at this things initially during investigation. One closer look and I found something, which got missed initially as we were focusing more on finding the serial killer.'

Mr. Paik did not give media the chance and asked 'What did you find Rajiv!'

'The belt, which Mr. Khan was wearing, like all other belts, had 5 holes to put the belt bucket in. But on this belt, there was another hole, which was manually created with the help of a screw driver of knife. It was quite far from the last (5th) hole. This manually created hole in the belt would tentatively have been the 8th hole if the belt manufacturers had not stopped at the 5th hole. This kind of improvisations are normally done in our middle class families so that the belt can be re-used by someone else or used longer, not by industrialists such as Mr. Khan. This could even damage their reputation. So, I immediately checked the pictures taken when his body was discovered and there, I could see that the belt bucket is logged in the 4th hole in the belt. But why? Why create a 8th hole if your size is the 4th hole. Why would a millionaire even use a belt, which is old and torn out and has an extra hole manually curved into it?'

'I could not make any headway from that findings and hence, I took the belt with me to Mr. Khan's wife and asked if it belonged to Mr. Khan. Mrs. Haseena Khan was adamant that this belt does not belong to Mr. Khan as he would never wear such belts. Mr. Khan was quite nitty about his style and fashion statement and always liked to wear branded dresses and would never wear a belt like this. I checked in her home that no one had the belt size for the 8th hole, so I could conclude that this belt most probably belongs to someone else, may be the killer! If the belt belongs to the murderer, why would he exchange the belt! The only logical explanation to that is the murderer exchanged his trousers with that of Mr. Khan.'

Someone beyond the flashlights of the media questioned 'Why would he do that?'

Rajiv answered 'May be because, when the killer killed Mr. Khan, the killer was wearing the light colored trouser which we found on Mr. Khan's body. The killing of Mr. Khan was a bloody affair and the blood must have spilt into the killer's trousers. If you remember, the murder happened in a highway where cabs are not available. If the murderer does not have a personal vehicle, he would have to use public transport and the murderer could not afford to go on a public transport with blood marks clearly visible in his trousers. So, he must have swapped it. Mrs. Haseena Khan had previously confirmed that Mr. Khan was wearing a black trouser when he left for the last time from his home. The blood must have spilt into Mr. Khan's trouser too but at night, it is very difficult to spot blood marks on a black trouser, so the killer exchanged the trousers after killing Mr. Khan.'

Mr. Paik exclaimed 'Oh my god, when did you find all of this Rajiv? Why did not you tell me? Did you check at Mr. Ghora's house about the trouser?'

Rajiv responded 'I was too busy with this findings and it was nothing conclusive. It could still be that I am stressing too much about the case and Mr. Ghora killed Mr. Khan but I just could not be satisfied with it. There are too many open questions to that. Also, please note that Mr. Ghora had confessed to be the serial killer and killing of Bikram Pal but he has never mentioned that he killed Mr. Khan. So, I always thought that there is more to this case and I was just investigating to confirm that we have looked at the case from every aspect and did not fall for someone's trap whereas this serial killer story was just used as a cover up. I just want to confirm that I have uncovered everything there is to it. I hope you understand and take no offence Mr. Paik.'

Mr. Paik nodded.

Again Rajiv resumed 'About Mr. Ghora, I took the same belt to Mr. Ashish Ghora's house and enquired the same. Mrs. Ghora confirmed that no one in the house wears such torn out belts with extra holes and Mr. Ashish Ghora was also very particular about his dressing style and would never wear such belts. So, the possibilities of Mr. Ghora killing Mr. Khan gets dimmer.'

Akash said 'Great going Rajiv, this are interesting clues, so did you find out anything more? May be Shankar has anything to do with it. Did you check his alibi?'

Rajiv said 'I did not, Akash, because he does not fit to the 'A.D' which Mr. Khan had written in his diary. The same A.D, whom Mr. Khan went to meet to Dharamshi Resort.'

Akash said 'May be he was using a false name!'

Rajiv said 'Or may be, A.D means 'Akash Detective' just as Mr. Dhole had mentioned on how people save phone numbers!'

Akash was again pissed 'Oh come on Rajiv, what's gotten into you! Why are you focused on linking me with everything?'

Rajiv said 'You remember Akash, the police belt I gifted you with a gun? I made sure that you wore the belt too! That was to check your belt size and it matches exactly in to the 8th hole of Mr. Samir Khan's belt. Shankar's waist fits only to the third hole. That's why I just can't get over the idea about you having something to do with this! Oh I forgot to mention, the gun and the gun license I gifted was fake too.'

Akash was lost for words, sensing that Rajiv played him last night.

One of the reporters stood up and echoed 'Just because a belt fits his size does not point anything at him! That is not a sufficient enough proof, why do you think that Akash has to do something with the Green Man?'

Rajiv turned away from the reporter and faced Akash 'Let me answer that one to you, Akash. I think you have something to do with this because your name in my guess work Sudoku box fills up maximum Sudoku boxes, like, I checked with Mr. Dhole again and asked him to stress and remember why he assigned you the part of the field to search near Hotel SMS where the body was found. He recalled and told me that after 30 minutes into searching, you had told him and I quote 'I have searched around a quarter of the field by the highways side and found nothing. I think we should split the team into sections so that we are more organized in the search. What do you think Mr. Dhole?' and then Mr. Dhole divided the work and assigned you the side where the body was found, because you had covered quite a lot of it. To me, that looks manipulative, Akash.'

Akash was stunned. He could only fumble 'I did not put that much thought into it Rajiv, it all happened as an accident. I did not plan and say it; it must have come out just like that!'

Rajiv calmly said 'I am not blaming you Akash, yet, but you must admit that your name in my Sudoku guess field solves most of my boxes, like, you had no appointment with Mr. Dhole the day Mrs Haseena Khan came to Mr. Dhole's police station. You had just came in to discuss your case with him. May be you followed Mrs Haseena and came to Mr. Dhole minutes before Mrs. Haseena Khan entered the police station. You had done your homework on Mr. Khan and continuously tried to impress her with your knowledge about the case despite Mr. Dhole's warnings. Oh! I also checked in your college about the project you talked about. Your college project on Mr. Khan. Apparently, you did not do any such project. Your project was on Global warming. You made the police look stupid, so that you can impress her. Mr. Dhole continuously tried to stop you but you did not stop until you got the case from Mrs. Haseena Khan.'

Akash erupted now 'Will you stop this bull shit Rajiv. What are you talking? Why would I do such a thing?'

Rajiv raised his voice too this time 'Because you needed to get inside the house to check if Mr. Khan has left a note of your name somewhere as you knew he has the habit of writing stuffs in his diary. This gives you the perfect excuse to go inside the house and check. You went and found out that he has only used your short form, he did not know your surname and so he used your profession to mark the appointment 'Akash Detective' – AD' but you made a mistake my friend, you should not have written 'S.M.S' yourself on the last page of the diary in Mr. Khan's room. An appointment is marked for a single place, not two places, Dharamshi Resort and Hotel S.M.S. If Mr. Khan knew that he was going to meet someone at Hotel S.M.S eventually, why would he write Dharamshi in the first place? Also, I got a handwriting expert check the word 'S.M.S' in Mr. Khan's diary and he has confirmed that it was not matching Mr. Samir Khan's handwriting.'

Everyone was stunned at this conversation and everyone was at a loss for words. Akash struggled to get words out of his mouth as he said 'Rajiv, I get it why you think I did it and it is logical too but you must trust me, I did not do any of these, I can swear on anybody, even my mother. Trust me Rajiv, I did not do any of these things. You cannot blame everything on me just because it fills your damn Sudoku board, you need to find out the truth and gather evidence.'

Rajiv again calmed down and said 'I know I need evidence Akash and hence I have already asked for the finger print report of Mr. Khan's trousers that I should have any moment now and then we can talk about evidence and see if I am right.'

Akash stammered 'But. But I have touched Mr. Khan's shirt and trousers at the murder site, you will surely find my fingerprints on them.'

Rajiv was again calm when he said 'Yes it should be on the outside of the trousers Akash or even the belt, but you should not have touched the inner side of the trousers in the murder site. I have asked to check for fingerprints on the top inner side of the trouser where the belt is worn, the side of the trouser, which is in touch with your hip. If any of us wants to open, his or her trouser, he or she must put their thumbs on the inside of the trouser where the belt is worn. I have asked for fingerprints from that part. The results should be with us any moment now. I have asked them to deliver it here.'

Akash laid down to his chair like a king who has lost his kingdom and stayed silent.

The media came to the rescue of its diminishing hero and questioned 'Why would Akash write anything about Hotel S.M.S in the diary knowing that anyone does not pen two appointment locations! And you had said that Mr. Shankar received a call from the serial killer, who called him?'

Rajiv said 'Now you are asking the right questions. If the fingerprint report confirms that my guess is right, then I will let Akash answer this question again. What I think is, and this is after the assumption that Akash is the killer; Akash knew that eventually police would discover the body of Mr. Khan and he may not be with the police at the crime scene to stage a story at that time. So, he came up with the story of the serial killer and planted the location of the dead body in the diary. He knew it was risky but he saw no other way of diverting the attention from the killer to a made up, serial killer. It was a risk that had to be taken so that he can be at the crime scene with the police and the reporters. I believe he called Shankar anonymously as Shankar was the only media reporter Akash knew of. When the reporters gathered as he had planned, he placed the first letter in the body, took it out himself and he enacted a stupidity and shouted about the serial killer so that it can be heard by the media and they market the news so that the hype gets created.'

Akash exclaimed 'Rajiv, now you are crossing the limit. How can you assume these things and that too, live, in front of the media and my mother? I am innocent and I was there with you the whole time when Mr. Ghora's car flipped in the highway. Why are you putting all of this on me Rajiv?'

Mr. Paik could not resist and stepped in 'Rajiv, I don't know what you are trying to get to but I can also vouch for Akash that he was hundreds of kilometers away from the crime scene of Mr. Ghora's car accident when it happened. I reached your hotel within an hour from the accident and Akash could not have been back from the accident site to the hotel within that time.'

CHAPTER 32

Rajiv looked to be in no hurry to respond. He was buying time for the fingerprints report to come in 'Of course he did not have anything to do with the murder of Mr. Ghora, Mr. Paik. Yourself, and I we are Akash's prime witness that can confirm that he did not have anything to do with Mr. Ghora's murder. If my thoughts are correct, that is exactly what Akash wanted? That is why he stayed with me at the hotel although his home is in the same city! He wanted a witness that can guarantee that he had nothing to do with the second victim, so that, he can happily be removed from the list of suspects for the serial killer.'

Mr. Paik was more surprised now 'Rajiv, you are confusing me now.'

Akash gave an expression, which suggested that he has given up on defending himself. One reporter demanded further explanation.

Rajiv obliged 'This question had been badgering me for days. The one question, which did not line with my Sudoku board at all. If Akash was the serial killer, how did he kill Mr. Ashish Ghora and why would Mr. Ghora confess to stage the car accident. I stressed and sweated to find a complex solution to my question but the answer lied in the simplicity of it. The answer is very simple; he was not at all involved in Mr. Ghora's car accident. Mr. Ghora himself staged the accident.'

After a theatrical pause to piss everyone, Rajiv continued 'During the murder of Mr. Khan, everything went as Akash had planned. After the public shaming during the court case of Damini's divorce, Akash stopped getting any clients for his detective endeavors. He was struggling to make ends meet. He realized that he might have to leave his dreams aside and go back to a desk job if things continued like this. Desk job was a nightmare to Akash and he would do everything in his power to stop that from happening. First, he must make some money to survive as he had no source of income and all his savings has been drained during the court case. That is when he thought about blackmailing Samir as he guessed that Samir's wife must not be aware of Samir's affair with Damini. He had hit jackpot when he found out that Samir is a very rich businessman and his wife is indeed not aware about Samir's affair. He called in to blackmail Samir. Samir got frightened and agreed to pay the initial demand and they were supposed to meet at Dharamshi Resort as per the note in Samir's appointment diary. If everyone can go a while back in their memory and remember, the night Samir was supposed to meet Akash at the Dharamshi Resort, there was a burglary of a gold shop in that area and it was packed with police. When Akash realized that the place is scramming with cops, he moved the appointment location to the isolated Hotel S.M.S. along the highway. Samir had already reached Dharamshi Resort when he received Akash's call and he too understood why the place was being changed and so he did not complain and agreed. Akash knew that blackmailing can prove to be a rough job and hence had carried a knife for self-protection. I can't guess how it went after that but somehow, Akash was driven with rage after meeting Samir, may be it had something to do with memories of Damini. Although he did not plan it during the blackmailing or changing the location to Hotel S.M.S, he must have got enraged at the sight of Mr. Khan. Or maybe Mr. Khan tried to attack Akash as he wanted the blackmailing to end. However it happened, during the unplanned tussle, Akash used his knife to kill Samir and during this tussle, his white trousers got lapped with red blood stains. As he would have to go back by public transport, he inter changed the trousers and wore Samir's dark colored one, dumped his body in the field and left the murder site. Please note that Akash was a well known face to public and would attract attention if people saw blood stains in his trousers.'

'Although Mrs. Haseena Khan did just what Akash wanted and hired him as the private detective for this case, the one thing that he did not plan for and could not stop was, Mrs. Haseena Khan emotionally branding Akash as the challenger for the serial killer. Akash must have chuckled a bit when he realized he was his own challenger. Nothing happened after that for few days as there was nothing to happen. There were no serial killer. It was all staged to cover up Mr. Khan's murder. But the news had spread across the country and it reached the ears of Mr. Ashish Ghora. Mr. Ghora knew that he was going to be sentenced for life and he was desperate to find a way out. Looking at the news, he found his escape route. He knew Akash was a Bengali and would be able to match the riddle with his Bengali surname, which means 'Horse'. Mr. Ghora was a hated personality across all Bengali household and so, Mr. Ghora rightly assumed that Akash would be aware of his name and his court case. So, he planted a riddle in Akash's house which would point to Mr. Ghora. He then waited for police to come to his doors so that he can be sure that the police has taken his bait. Once he got the news from his wife that the police was looking for him, he executed his plan of the car accident and killed Bikram Pal. Now, just think about all of this from Akash's perspective. He receives a note from the same serial killer, which he himself had enacted. So, from the first moment, he knew it was fake and he wanted to use it to his own advantage. He knew that there is going to be some action very soon and if he can get myself and Mr. Paik to vouch for him and say that Akash was nowhere near the accident site and could not have anything to do with the murder, he would never be linked to the Green Man. When we went to the crash site, Akash very well knew that this was not the act of any serial killer but someone else was staging this for their own personal gains. I later on went to check the pictures from the burnt body of Bikram Pal and found no fortune rings in the corpse's fingers. We had gathered from Mrs. Ghora that Mr. Ashish Ghora strongly believed in astrology and wore multiple fortune rings. As we were obsessed with the serial killer we missed that point then but from the missing fortune rings, Akash straight away understood that this was not Mr. Ghora and Mr. Ghora has staged his own murder.'

Mr. Paik said 'Shit! Really! We were so much focused on the Green Man that we did not doubt the case and dig through! Fuck!'

Akash finally broke his silence 'Is there any proof to all this Rajiv or you are just going to continue explaining your fantasy to all of us!'

Rajiv straightened 'This are not crimes Akash that I can charge you with, I will give proofs for my fantasies when the time comes. If you all kindly remember, I was struggling to fit in, why would Mr. Ashish Ghora not kill Debasis Sen in the Warehouse and instead, puke the truth out to him! If he had a gun to shoot Akash, why did he not shoot Debasis? Also, Debasis confirmed that he could not find a gun on Mr. Ashish Ghora' Again a theatrical pause 'may be because it was hidden!' a pause again and then 'Or maybe he did not carry a gun!'

The sound of the room gave away everyone's surprise at Rajiv's deductions. The media shouted back 'Then how did he shoot Akash!'

Rajiv faced towards Akash with a rugged smile 'Akash! What are they asking! How were you shot! Will you answer?'

Akash gave an angry look towards Rajiv and said 'Everyone knows that Rajiv, I had just now explained'

Rajiv spoke 'Then explain me this Akash, why were all the exit doors locked for the Warehouse! With a lock, which looks brand new, whereas the warehouse was closed down years ago! All exit doors, except one. When you had suddenly shouted at Shankar holding the camera and messed up our plan, in the heat of the moment, suddenly, you took charge and asked all of us to scramble to other exits where as you directed yourself to cover the only exit, which was unlocked.'

'That was my bad luck Rajiv, I did not know that it was the only one unlocked and about the locks, you need to ask the owner, why are you asking me! You know very well, I shouted to save you, to save you from someone I thought was going to take your life and this is how you repay me! By insulting me in front of everyone and even my mother! It was the heat of the moment and no one took charge, so I had to take charge and position you all to other exits. If you had taken the charge at that moment, I would not have to.'

'Ok Akash, we found Mr. Ghora's body at around 20 feet away from the door and we found you by the exit door. So, when Mr. Ghora shot you, he must have been around 15 feet away from you!'

'Mmmmmm, he was a bit far from me and that's why his shot did not hit my heart, where he had aimed for, yes 15 feet, it should be.'

'So, both the shots fired were at around 15 feet or more from the target?'

'Yes, should be'

'But this forensic report says that both the shots were fired at point blank range, only a few inches from the body!'

Akash looked stunned now 'I.... I.... I really don't know how Raj....'

Mr. Paik stepped in 'Wow Rajiv! When did you find this out? Why did you not tell me? So, the forensic report does not match with Akash's story!'

Rajiv looked up at Mr. Paik and gave an expression with his eyes, further to which he did not need to answer back to Mr. Paik. Then he turned to the media and said 'That is the difference between a private detective and a police officer. We can think through all the loopholes of a story and take help of the forensic reports to prove our theories, which a private detective cannot. Now let me reveal another finding from the forensic report. The gun that was used to shoot at Akash, does not have the fingerprints of Mr. Ashish Ghora. I mean there are fingerprints of only 2 fingers of Mr. Ghora on the gun and that too on the barrel, not on the trigger or on the handle, so, we can safely assume that Mr. Ghora did not fire that gun. Akash, you fired it on yourself, using your handkerchief on your right hand to shoot your left arm in a point blank distance and then placed the gun's barrel under the fingers of Mr. Ghora.'

Akash looked blank and stooped his head down. Mr. Paik had a look of disbelief about him but he hurriedly positioned his officers on the dais beside Akash so that he cannot make any sudden moves.

The media asked the obvious 'Officer! Where are you going with this, how was this setup? And why would Akash shoot himself?'

Rajiv said 'Let's resume from the car accident then. Once Akash knew that Mr. Ghora has enacted as the Green Man, he figured out that it would be a great chance for him to end this episode forever and pin everything on Mr. Ashish Ghora. But to do that, he needs to ensure that Mr. Ghora does not open his mouth about Samir Khan's murder. So, Akash has to silence him forever so that he can die as the Green Man. Akash somehow contacted Mr. Ghora and blackmailed him saying that he knew that he was alive and they needed to meet. He fixed the spot as an abandoned warehouse and locked all the exit points except one at the back. Now he sent a letter to himself, the second letter so that the police can be evidently present at the warehouse and he can carry out his plan of eliminating Mr. Ghora forever under the shadow of the police, in the name of justice. But, he needed a third victim, to make it look as if the Green Man has plotted for his third murder and the police are stopping it. So, he calls up Debasis and lures him to come to the warehouse at the same time as he had called Mr. Ghora. Now, all he needs is a distraction, so he phones up Shankar and lures him to come to the site too. Mr. Ghora was running for his life and he did not have any gun with him, so he did not attempt to kill Debasis. Just when we were about to go inside the warehouse to catch the Green Man, aka Mr. Ashish Ghora, Akash created a diversion by shouting at Shankar whereas he knew that he was holding only a camera. Once the diversion was created and we were short staffed, we only had few seconds to come up with plan B and at that time, Akash put forward his plan and we abided by it. Actually, we were falling in his trap. He had sent us all to closed exits whereas he made his way to the only open exit. He then went passed the door and hid around 15 feets from the door under a tree in the darkness. As Mr. Ghora came out of the exit and towards the boundary wall, he creeped near him and from his back, fired a shot using the police rifle at his left belly, knowing fully well that it was going to be a fatal shot. He did not go for the head shot as it would not look realistic for a first timer. Akash had brought a second rifle with him and now, he pulls out a second rifle with a handkerchief, fires it on himself and puts it by Mr. Ghora and runs back towards the door and lays down.' Rajiv was getting more and more excited as he got near the end and after finishing his last statement, he rose up and proudly said 'And that's a wrap, case closed. He knew that he would be a hero if he was shot and no one would ever doubt him further and that is exactly what happened. You reporters went crazy over him although you did not know the facts.'

Then he triumphantly looked at Akash and said 'Am I right Akash! Did I miss anything? Great plan, I must say it was a great plan and would have fooled me too if only I had not come across the belt in Samir Khan's trousers'

Akash did not dare look up and kept silent.

Mr. Paik proudly got up and started clapping at Rajiv. Few seconds ahead, the other officers joined in too and finally, further few seconds onwards, the media finally joined in. The whole room was clapping for Rajiv except Akash. Akash looked up to see his mother's reaction but his heart broke as he saw the seat to be empty, he sulked down again.

Everyone knows the police are always late to arrive everywhere. This was no exception. Once the claps were over, a police officer came to Rajiv with the forensic reports and presented it to Rajiv. Rajiv looked at the reports and beamed with a smile. He then showed the report to everyone and said 'Turns out that my Sudoku board guess was right and it is now complete. Akash, you are under arrest for the murder of Mr. Samir Khan and Mr. Ashish Ghora. You wanted proof, here you go, all the forensic reports prove the charges I am pressing on you.'

CHAPTER 33

Two weeks later, Mr. Paik invited Rajiv to his home for dinner, a treat for saving the police's ass and uncovering the twisted truth that brought Akash to justice. Akash was in police custody. He confessed and fell in to Rajiv's Sudoku board as the evidences were too strong. He confessed that he had no intentions to kill Mr. Khan initially, but when they went to Hotel S.M.S., Mr. Khan ushered a gun at him and wanted to kill Akash and end the blackmailing forever. Akash had indeed brought a kitchen knife for self-defense. He kneeled down and pleaded for apologies to Mr. Khan who was shaking to shoot with the gun as Mr. Khan was not proficient with it. As Mr. Khan came closer to shoot, Akash branded his knife out in a flash and pushed it inside the belly of Mr. Khan. Mr. Khan fell down and was screeching in pain. Akash was already enraged with the thought of Mr. Khan having sex with Damini and her moaning in pleasure. This thought, toppled with the reality that Mr. Khan tried to kill him drove him crazy and he stabbed the injured Mr. Khan multiple times out of rage. He took Mr. Khan's gun with him when he left the murder spot and used the same gun on himself in Rhino Warehouse. He had used one of his connections to get a phone number which cannot be traced back and used that to call Shankar during Mr. Khan's murder case at Hotel S.M.S and also to bring Shankar to Rhino Warehouse

The media had shifted their alliance from Akash to Rajiv. Rajiv was the talk of the town now and the videos of him setting up Akash to his Sudoku board in front of 50 media reporters had gone viral. He was nick named 'Sudoku Raj' by youthful Indians all across and he was awarded a medal of honor by the Indian Government for cracking the complex case and stopping Akash from making a fool out of the police force. After dinner, Mr. Paik poured some JD in to a glass for both of them and said 'Cheers to your Sudoku board, Rajiv. You are one bad ass with logic. How could you see through the case so easily! Akash had us properly fooled and I would have never suspected him, ever. How did you do it?'

Rajiv gave a calm smile and said 'It's nothing! It's just that the story was not fitting, I just could not live peacefully with what was showcased to us as the truth. There were small loop holes through out which did not match but we were so busy with the Green Man, we never had the time to think about any other angle. The biggest hole, which actually made me think the most, was the one in the belt. But trust me, it's going on wild now. I have always hated cameras and now its all over me. I just hope this gets over quickly and our public finds a new thing to cheer about. I am sure it's not far, may be a day or two more.'

'A day or two! You have been trending for two weeks now. It isn't gonna be over soon Rajiv. Be prepared to be in the limelight for 2 weeks more at the least.'

'Fuck it man, I really get embarrassed when I see the video of the press conference that day. I looked so stupid sometimes.'

Mr. Paik rejoiced 'Who cares about your stupid face, the only thing I love about the video is Akash's face. The way his expressions change. He keeps on fighting for some time till you have him cornered, you deliver the final stab, and then you should look at him. That expression on his face was priceless. Did you see that?'

'I wasn't looking at Akash at all during the conference, Mr. Paik'

'Then what were you looking at? Your nemesis – the cameras!' Mr. Paik

'My nemesis indeed. You should have looked at her face Mr. Paik. It was horrifying. With my every blow, her face just crumbled with sadness and I could not take it anymore. I hoped I could stop, stop hurting her this much but my hands were tied, I had to bring her son to justice.'

'You mean Akash's mother?'

'Who else! You are lucky that you did not have to look into her eyes. A mother can never curse anyone. Mothers are too loving to do that but I could sense that she desperately wanted to make me stop, she wanted to save her son but she could not do anything. Initially, she thought I was trying to frame her son, she looked at me with fiery eyes that can engulf anyone. I could not match eyes with her and so I stared elsewhere. Then, as I slowly started drilling my cards and she slowly started to take in that his son may be at fault, she looked at me with pleading eyes that urged me to stop harassing her son but I had my hands tied, I could not stop. During the end of the conference, even before I had proved that Akash was guilty, she looked at Akash once and in that one look, her motherly instincts knew that she was the mother of a murderer and she could not take it anymore. She got up from her seat and vanished. I had signaled a havildar to go after her and later on the havildar reported that she laid down on the pavement and just stared at the sky, for close to an hour and then she just went home. But those eyes, I just cannot forget those disappointed eyes and how much it wanted to hurt me, to stop me and save her son. But she knew that I was doing the right thing and she knew that her son was guilty but she struggled to accept it.

'Why did you disclose all of this in front of the media? Why not in an interrogation room?'

'I thought about it Mr. Paik, I thought about it so many times over that. Would it be the correct move to do this in the press conference? But if I had not done that, everyone would have thought that the police are too jealous of Akash and we are forging up evidences and setting him up. If I did not break his popular image, we would have a bunch of supporters cheering for him outside the police station and every newspaper questioning how we had trapped a common man and put all the blame on him. All the proofs we would provide would be noted as a setup and no one would believe that their hero, who took a bullet to save them from a serial killer, had actually plotted one of the smartest murder plot that Indian police has ever come across.'

'Yes that's true, I understand and agree, and that is how it would have been but you out smarted the smartest murder plot, I would drink to that' Mr. Paik raised his glass and gulped.

Rajiv smiled and said 'Cheers'

Mr. Paik finished his glass and said 'I understand your feelings about his mother. Indeed a nasty act. I will find the culprit who called his mom to the press conference and give him a piece of my shit'

'Is that absolutely necessary? Your shit? If affirmative, then you have that culprit right in front of you!'

Mr. Paik looked disarrayed now 'You bastard, you called his mom to make him weak and confess! You used his mom against him. You will rot in hell for that!'

'Hell is where my wife's gonna be too. So, my afterlife does not look much promising.'

Mr. Paik's house echoed of their laughter.

www.ingramcontent.com/pod-product-compliance
Ingram Content Group UK Ltd.
Pitfield, Milton Keynes, MK11 3LW, UK
UKHW042018190726
13854UKWH00005B/2350

9 788194 544562